FOODMARES:
The Crazy, Food
Induced Dreams of
Dashel Gabelli

Nadrio —

Here ya go! A limited edition copy of a most AMAZING book! when it becomes a movie, it might be worth enough to buy a pack of smokes — the generic kind that are made from corn husks on Indian reservations and have been banned in every state — And Puerto Rico!!

Dashel Gabelli

2/5/02

FOODMARES:
The Crazy, Food Induced Dreams of Dashel Gabelli

Dashel Gabelli

Writers Club Press

San Jose   New York   Lincoln   Shanghai

FOODMARES:
The Crazy, Food Induced
Dreams of Dashel Gabelli

Writers Club Press
an imprint of iUniverse, Inc.

For information address:
iUniverse, Inc.
5220 S. 16th St., Suite 200
Lincoln, NE 68512
www.iuniverse.com

ISBN: 0-595-21217-4

Printed in the United States of America

I would like to dedicate this work of pure pseudo-research to all those who eat a lot, sleep a lot, and come up with the most interesting of dreams! God Love Ya!

Acknowledgments

One would think that in the 20 years or so that it took to create this magnificent work of study, there would exist numerous individuals to whom I should extend a degree of thanks. You would think that. However, that is not the case. I understand that I carry with me the stigma of never completing anything that I start and that alone would be a compelling enough reason for anyone not to get too excited when I announced that I was working on this project in the first place. And I'm sure that any excitement anyone may have had would have waned immensely when reports of progress came in time periods of years rather than days, weeks or even months. Even the announcement that the work was nearing completion brought with it very little to none in the ways of encouragement. This being the case, I have had to spend quite a bit of time to try and find anyone who I could even remotely consider as actually having helped or encouraged me in any way at any time along the way. The list is rather short.

The first individual I would like to extend a measure of gratitude is Mylan Jones of Omaha, Nebraska. Mr. Jones allowed me, after much begging and pleading, to operate his newly acquired farm combine–a large, tractor—like device used in the harvesting of wheat and such–for an afternoon. I must say that I truly enjoyed the experience, navigating this behemoth across hundreds and hundreds of magnificent amber waves of grain—and soybeans, and some other stuff that I just plain never seen before!

How did this help with my project? Good question. It didn't, but he seemed like a nice enough fellow, allowing a person he barely knew to take one of the most expensive and necessary pieces of farm equipment out for a "Sunday drive." Thank you, Mylan Jones! I am sure that a few straight years of abundant harvests will more than cover any damage I may have caused to your machine, pick up truck, barn, silo, livestock, and living area. I hope you get out of jail soon (I thought you would know that shooting at people, such as myself, with a shotgun is against the law—no matter that I happened to ignore your multiple warnings shouted over a mega-decibel bullhorn while riding by my side in a pick up truck) so you can get those crops planted and start to recoup your losses!

I would also like to thank Daphne Wentworth, president of the Pregnant Gals of Pennsylvania (PGOP) for allowing me to attend several luncheons where I was able to observe, first hand, the exaggerated feeding frenzy of pregnant women and attempting to interview them about their dreams. It was such a marvel to see and I wish that they would do away with the rule that prohibits "image capturing" (i.e. photography, videos, sketch artistry, caricatures, etc.) at their events. Though from I have seen at these luncheons, I can well imagine that these individuals would certainly not want their pictures taken as they pounced on buffet table like it was a wounded gazelle and they were hungry lions. I nearly was knocked unconscious when three women who, obviously from their size were well into their pregnancies, charged the serving table when the roast pig was rolled out. These magnificent women all clawing and grabbing and chewing of the heavily fat laden food were truly something to behold! Ever wonder why there has never been a documentary about this phenomenon? Me too. I suppose something like that is okay for animal shows, but I suppose that it would make your stomach turn if you saw human beings doing the same.

So, thank you, Daphne, for all your patience and understanding–and for not calling the police over that little incident which we are both aware of and will not go into here. All I will say, however, is that for future reference you may want to refrain from referring to your guests at such events as "someone who wants to see how you gals make pigs of yourselves when you eat." It was inevitable that these women would take offense to such an announcement and quite understandable that they might launch an "offensive" against such an individual and, conversely, it can only be expected that such an individual would indeed launch a "counter attack" which can only leave a tremendous mess and unspecified damages which could total quite a bit of money in the restaurant. Again...thanks!

Lastly, but certainly not leastly (yeah, I know it's not a word, I like the way it sounds, relax, you don't have to go check your dictionaries), I would like to acknowledge the individuals I have had the great pleasure of "meeting" on the Internet. Countless hours of chatting when I should have been doing my job has, I believe, caused my brain to turn into a sloppier grade of mush than it was to begin with. However, I would like to extend a special thanks to the "nagger." Without your continual whining and nagging day in and day out, week after week for a hell of a long time, I might have not have finished this as fast as I did. With all that nagging, I would guess that you saved me maybe a couple of weeks tops. Even your best efforts could never overcome my fear of actually completing something. But, thank you nonetheless.

I have finished the book. The nagging has stopped. I suppose that I shouldn't even mention that I have started another.

Dashel Gabelli
Orlando, Florida
December 6, 2001

SECTION I
What's It All About, Dash?

When I first began telling people that I was on the verge of completing a book that through years of research shows a direct correlation between the foods I have eaten before sleep and the detailed and vivid dreams they produced, they all replied, "That's nice. Who are you?" I then went and told the same to people I actually knew and their reply was along the lines of, "Really?! That's just great! Another book that tries to interpret people's dreams. I can't wait for it to come out. You be sure and let me know when it does, okay? If you can find me, that is. Jackass."

"Aha!" I would remark, with my index finger in the air and my brows arched upwards. I would then go on to explain that my book in no way attempts (well, maybe in some cases, but those are half-assed attempts at best) to interpret dreams, but rather recalls the dreams that I have had after consuming various combinations of foods. How by mixing and blending the base chemicals found on the molecular level of all foods, I was able to produce the visions that danced across my eyelids when I drifted off to sleep at night or even just collapsed in a food induced (and sometimes alcohol, too!) coma into an easy chair or the exceptionally hard concrete floor of my cluttered garage.

Well, this seemingly ridiculous (to my acquaintances, not to me, of course) statement seemed to touch off a rash of harsh conversation, questioning my capabilities, abilities, and just about everything else, to actually do something that in anyway at all could possible resemble or otherwise be misconstrued as "research." Questions such as, "Who are you kidding?! When did you do this research? Between naps?" "Of course you're capable of doing scientific research. Did you know I was the guy in the R2D2 suit in the Star Wars movies?" and "Oh, yeah, right, you did research. You're that guy who taught that chicken to play tic-tac-toe, weren't you? Damn, I saw you on the TV. You's a regular scientist!" abounded. The harshest criticism came from my closest "friend."

"Oh, I see. You, Dashel Gabelli, with one entire year of advanced education, during which you spent the majority of your time playing pranks in the dorm elevators, watching The Wheel of Fortune and reruns of The Waltons instead of attending classes and making long distance calls to foreign countries and charging them to the room of the goofy kid from Alabama, have acquired the strong theoretical and practical disciplines necessary to consider yourself a man of science?"

"Well…" I started

"No, wait. Let me get this straight," he continued in his tinny and sarcastic whine, "You have been able to conduct controlled tests, including sufficient 'double-blind' ones, to produce results that would stand up under the intense scrutiny of the scientific community? You have had your data audited by accredited specialists that will attest to the adherence of various scientific protocols and would be willing to verify strict disciplines were maintained to a panel of respected members of the research world?"

"Well, not actually. You see…" I would again attempt to rebut this vicious attack of words.

"So what your are telling me, Dash, my friend, is that you are a great man that has been able to deliver to the world amazing and utterly irrefutable results of magnificent 'experiments'?"

"It's like this…." I managed to get in before again being slammed.

"Please, oh great Dashel, tell me what it's like. What's it all about, Dash?"

It appeared that my best friend, the super gifted, super smart science guy was miffed that I could actually do anything requiring any level of education past the 11th grade. I believe that he was still somewhat bitter that his recent experiments in tick and flea repellents as well as his great studies in the carbonation of dairy products were soundly dismissed as horrible failures. He was never quite able to combine his potent potion that eradicates the problem of flea and ticks forever and a proper method of delivery. The pill he developed was the size and shape of a pack of cigarettes and was exceptionally difficult for animals to ingest and, if they actually did manage to swallow the enormous pill (with the help of high pressure air and a garden hose), to digest as well. It also caused the poor, pitiful beasts to shrink. In his lab he has a St. Bernard dog the size of a small frog.

And his effort to bring to all the people of the world a carbonated cheese drink was also unsuccessful. He had not been able to find a way to keep cheddar (and every other cheese as well) in a blended and suspended state that would not cause individuals to choke and vomit. Anyways, who would want to drink a cheese soda?

"Millions of people, dammit! Millions I tell you!!" he shouted into a tremendous sound amplification system, that was specifically manufactured for the rock group "The Who," at a some mediocre science symposium (the meeting facility managed to buy the extremely loud equipment from an online auction site for a bargain since it was mislabeled as an amplification system once used by Weird Al Yancovich) when someone actually asked a similar question during the early phases of his experimentation.

"Just imagine," he continued, "being able to slip a few coins or a perfectly straight, unwrinkled, clean dollar bill into a vending machine and extract a delectable and extremely refreshing 'Cheddar Cola' or a frosty, thirst slaying 'Nacho Man Tonic!' It's killer, I tell ya, killer!!"

Yeah, I'm sure. The room had virtually emptied when he was first announced as the speaker and the remainder had left a few moments after he shouted out "Millions…" so I can understand that his embarrassment and frustration might compel him to be a bit harsh with mention of research completed by myself.

Well, in any event, I felt that even though I had informed him (he was my best friend after all) of my research as I was compiling the information, I should perhaps give him again the explanation from the beginning. To go over how this thing started and fill him in on my studies and the levels of science I utilized. I didn't have much practical (or impractical) background in Science…. or Math or English or for anything academic for that matter, but ask me on how to bamboozle the long distance operator into reverse charging a call to Botswana or New Zealand, and I am a genius! But, I felt compelled to defend myself.

First of all, the last thing I profess to be is a man who has come up with great scientific revelations. My entire scientific experimental experience can be summarized by the one day in Chemistry class (which I failed miserably) when the exceptionally large teacher (a behemoth of a man with a beard that wore flannel shirts and had a penchant for regaling his captured audience with long-winded stories of his long bow and 12 gauge shotgun hunting escapades) told us to sniff the open bottle of ammonia he had circulating among the students.

Now, I, again claiming ignorance in the arena of science, didn't think that this little demonstration would amount to anything. I also believed that the extent of any injury would be minimal. It was, after all, a high school Chemistry class. After several of the students, perhaps having seen this stunt before (we did have some individuals who failed the previous year, and lacking any sensibility whatsoever, decided to retake the class…. dopes!) passed on the "sniffing" of the liquid, one brave soul attempted to "capture" the fumes in a way that students who actually pay attention to science teachers do—by gently wafting a cupped hand over the open vessel and cautiously try to detect a hint of aroma.

The effect was…nothing. He said he smelled nothing and that he "suffered no ill effects—at least at the superficial, external level, though a thorough physical and psychological examination would be required to rule out any damage to the delicate tissue, cellular corruption or even mental facility degeneration." Egghead. Poindexter. By the way, this once intense student of Chemistry is now in charge of ties, handkerchiefs and boxer shorts (and sometimes even wallets—only the discontinued, vinyl models, mind you) at the local "Worn and Slightly Soiled and/or Stained" clothing and large shoe outlet store. He also sells models of ships, office buildings and bridges that he manufactures from the numerical keys of discarded calculators at the flea market twice a month.

Midway through his summation of the cause and effect relationship (yes, he continued to drone on after the previous statement) of chemical toxins and body material, I tapped him on the shoulder and said, "Shut the hell up, Brainiac 2000, and pass me the freakin' bottle already!" He smiled and gave it to me.

The next thing I can clearly recall is waking up on the cold terrazzo floor of the classroom and overhearing the teacher and the Egghead discussing the need for more stringent safety procedures in science classes. I could only assume they were referring to me. My head was pounding and my eyes seemed to have dried up like a couple of Spanish Olives that had been sitting on the hors d'oeuvres tray for several hours.

"You see," began the teacher, standing on his hind legs (looking a lot like one of those decrepit dancing and juggling bears they have at fourth rate carnivals), "Ammonia doesn't affect everyone the same way. Some individuals don't even smell the distinct aroma, which is why some students will come into school reeking like a horde of damn cats that went on a spraying spree. On the other hand, people like yourself can suffer a debilitating trauma. See how fun Chemistry can be?"

Everyone had a good laugh at my expense as I was assisted to the Nurses Office where she game me two un-buffered, children's chewable (grapefruit flavored!) aspirin and a small container (the kind with the aluminum foil lid that your tear off) of pseudo—pasteurized and unfiltered lemon juice.

After my failing Chemistry, the following year I took a cheesy class titled "Some Science You Can Use If You Have To" which dealt with day to day science and how it is used. I was the king of the class when I unleashed my Ammonia Experiment!

As I told this part of my story to my scientist friend, he merely commented, "Serves you right for trying to mess with Science, punk bastard!"

Having no idea what he was talking about, I went on to explain that my extent of Psychological knowledge (he and others still have the impression that I am a dream analyst though I keep informing them that I am no such thing—screw 'em for not paying attention) was even less than that of Science. It borders on virtually nil. The only actual encounter with the study of the mind that I have experienced occurred when a pop psychologist was on an afternoon talk show. He was all smiles trying to explain, while constantly trying to readjust his red ascot and red hair piece, in simplistic terms how wonderful it is to release bad, embedded experiences in ones past and to live a free and clear life when I inadvertently knocked over our new 19" color TV. The TV exploded and my Mother broke several wooden soupspoons on my ass. That was it. Then we bought a new TV a few days later. I was not allowed within 15 feet of the new purchase. My extent of psychological knowledge.

So how does a very curious kid, with no real ambition to learn Science or Psychology or Math or any subject —other than to know how to spell them properly—do to entertain himself? Right! He immerses himself in the most amazing world of trivia! Tons and tons of nonsensical, anecdotal tidbits of information that would only come in handy in Trivial Pursuit (never lost a game) or on a game show (never tried to get on one—too much actual work involved; like picking up the phone, dialing, actually talking, etc.). To my surprise, however, this is the field of knowledge that sparked my dream research. How? Well…

On a hot afternoon when I was 18 years old and just loafing around the house (it was summertime—too hot to go outside, too lazy to go to work—as if I had a job anyway) and watching cartoons and commercials on how I can feed an entire village of filthy, shoeless, poor children for only 13 cents a day (THAT's where I need to shop!!) or those that tell me on how to become a Medical Transcriptionist or a Small Engine Mechanic at home in my spare time, I glanced at my bookshelf and suddenly decided that I would finish the book I had recently bought. "The Stuff That Will Just Plain Make Your Head Explode: All You Ever Wanted To Know About Nothing In Particular." You have to admit, with a title like that, it screams to be read.

I started out by reading a couple of short, insignificant essays on some "amazing" individuals who were only classified as such due to their unique physical abnormalities or simply because they possess a highly unusual behavioral trait. Like being able to eat large hunks of irradiated metal or have the innate talent of being able to ingest several pounds of dirt a day—without milk or any liquid at all—and remain regular. Now that is truly amazing!

Jumping ahead a few pages, I found myself in the section of the book that dealt with "Statistical Trivia and Other Fun Facts." Incredible stuff like a jellyfish is 95% water. Wow. The next tidbit stated that an elephant is the only mammal that cannot jump. I tried to think back in my memory banks if there ever was a time that I witnessed (live or on TV) an elephant jump. I couldn't think of any such occurrence and, pondering further, surmised that this indeed was correct as the image of an enormous beast trying to simply hop was a ludicrous one.

Continuing on, I discovered in this wonderful book that a toothpick is the object most often choked upon by Americans. Well, that sounded plausible, though I did wonder why it was only Americans. Do we care more about dental hygiene than other countries? I was more than a bit interested in finding out what was the object most choked upon by Canadians, but that interest quickly faded as I read the next mind boggling item. According to this book, in Tokyo, Japan, they sell toupees for dogs. Toupees? I thought they ate dogs in Japan. I immediately adjusted my mental "junk drawer" and corrected myself by recollecting that it was in Korea (Both North and South) that they ate dogs. I think. Nevertheless, I couldn't fathom any one buying a toupee for a dog. I started to seriously doubt the credibility of the book.

Reading on, the book stated that—as an indisputable fact—Babe Ruth wore a cabbage leaf under his cap to keep himself cool. He changed it every two innings. Hmmmm. This sounded so unbelievably ridiculous that it was probably true. Babe was a bit of booze hound and known for his crazy quirks, so I imagine nothing he did seemed out of place. But, being the role model and idol he was, I was a bit surprised that I had never heard of a run on cabbage leaves as hordes of children would have demanded—with lots of screaming, yelling and threatening to hold their breaths until they died—that their parents let them adorn their noggins with the leaf that "Babe Wears." Anyways, I read on.

Immediately following that was the "fact" that 2/3rds of all Eggplant in the world is grown in New Jersey (possibly a vegetable theme emerging). That was possible. How much could 2/3rds of the world's eggplant supply actually be? 100, maybe 200? I don't know anyone who eats eggplant—or at least admits to doing so (though it is one of the items I have ingested during my research phase). Still, that credibility thing was being stretched.

I was about to put the book down when I caught the next "Fun Fact." The average person has over 1460 dreams per year. Well, the first thing that astounded me was that instead of giving us the actual number, they say it's "over" 1460. What is it? 1461? 1465? 5718? What? Why can't you just tell me the exact number? Then something flashed in my mind that was profound. The average person has one thousand four hundred and sixty plus dreams a year. I consider myself to be an "average" person (in spite of what my friends, family, children from foreign countries and every other individual I run into tell me) and I can't for the life of me remember maybe more than a handful or so of dreams in my lifetime (remember, I'm only 18 at the time). Yet I am supposed to have had over 1460 dreams a year. And who counted the dreams? And if you're like me and can't recall much of any dreams, how would you know how many I actually had? All this "factual" information was now bordering on the absurd. I had to find out if the junk contained in this book had any merit.

I found the telephone number of the publisher and called to find out if I could, well, find out something about these apparently bizarre "facts." Much to my surprise, I was directed to a company spokesperson in very short order. She told me that I was not the only person to call and check on some of the info that they put into the book. In fact, I was informed that there had been over 513 calls so far. Exactly how many, I inquired.

"Over 513, sir," she replied.

"Yeah, I know. You said that already. I want to know EXACTLY the number of callers there have been," I said.

"That would be over 513, sir," she droned in a monotone.

"How many over? Two or 3500 over?" I persisted.

"Are you on medication? Are you stoned or something?" she asked.

I quickly dropped the numbers game after assuring her that, no, I was not a mental deficient and that I have not been medicated for any types of psychological disorders nor have I taken any legal/illegal drugs with in the last 48 hours. "But you should have seen me three days ago! WOOHOO, what a mess I was then!" She didn't see the humor. I quickly went on with a litany of questions I had written down on a piece of the back cover of the King of Prussia/Valley Forge (Pennsylvania) Yellow Pages.

She was good. She had the definitive answer to all my questions, providing me with bibliographies and assorted resources to do independent confirmations on my own. When I inquired about the dream stats, she said, "First of all, don't do that number asking crap again, or this conversation is over!" before going on to give me numerous resources to validate the numbers and anything else in regards to this dream stuff I could ever want. Now I was getting excited. I wanted to find out what this stuff was all about!

I told her that she was most helpful and that I was deeply appreciative of all the time and effort she gave in answering my queries.

"Get clean and get a job," she told me before hanging up the phone.

I immediately jumped into the rust bucket Ford Maverick that I was never proud to call my own (but it did have four wheels and an engine—that worked! All at the same time!!), and headed down to the county library in Norristown, PA to start my "research."

In the library, I quickly went around in an attempt to collect all the resource materials I could. Never fully understanding the highly complex mechanics of the Dewey Decimal System and suddenly suffering a bout of laziness, I was only able to find one reference book and a series of articles that were published in a Psychological publication. Nearly at the brink of exhaustion, I found an empty table and sat myself down in the chair and put my head down for a second or two.

When I raised my head, I saw that sitting across from me was a guy with a toothpick dangling from the corner of his mouth, looking at me. He looked kind of goofy—about thirty something and one of those annoying smiles that those crazy, super happy people or the mentally infirm tend to sport. He seemed harmless enough.

"Hey, how are ya, kid? I'm Frankie B. I'm the smartest man in Nebraska," he started.

Oh, Boy, here we go, I thought to myself.

"Hey, Frankie B," I said while extending out my right hand, "I'm Dash."

"Yeah, nice to meet you," he started again, ignoring my outstretched hand, making me feel like an ass, "I might be able to help you what with ya got there."

"Well, I'm just doing a little research on..." I said before being cut off.

"Hey, ya wanna know how I became the smartest man in Nebraska?" he asked, not really wanting an answer.

"Yeah, sure, go ahead," I replied the only answer I felt would satisfy his question.

He took the toothpick out of his mouth, took a breath, and began his saga.

He began by restating his name, "It's Frankie B. That's it, understand?" and telling me that he was originally a second rate carpenter that lived in Missouri. He held about 6 or 7 jobs with different contractors, losing his job each time for talking too much. He told me that he had so much important information "crammed in this incredibly efficient head of mine" that he had to repeatedly spew his words of wisdom and profound knowledge to his co-workers nonstop. Everyday. I would have fired him too, I thought to myself. Either that or shoot him. He was beginning to mildly irritate me.

He said that one day, one of his bosses had gotten extremely upset with him and just began shouting at Frankie B in front of everybody. Frankie B, obviously so embarrassed at such a turn of events, he felt he had to take revenge. He said he walked into the nearly rusted out employee trailer that sat on cement blocks and "teetered like a see saw when you went from one side to the other," opened the mold covered refrigerator and took out a Charleston Chew candy bar that had been in the freezer for several months and headed back out to confront his boss.

"I didn't mean to kill him, you see, but I swung that frozen piece of caramelized sugar and preservatives so hard it cracked my boss' hard hat," Frankie B told me, rather nonchalant, "and, well, it cracked his head as well."

"Wait a minute!" I whispered extremely loud, "You killed someone?"

"Well, actually, I found out several years later that he only needed one stitch to cover the nearly superficial cut over his eyebrow that he received when I unleashed my mighty strength against his hat with that candy bar. But, at the time, I believed that I had killed him!" replied Frankie B.

Frankie B continued on, informing me that he took it on the lam. He went home, packed up a few shirts and pants and all his tools, loaded up his fantastic pick up that "starts every time, if you give it just a little bit of gas and rub the dashboard in a circular motion, not too hard, mind you, just nice and easy" and headed out of state.

He quickly skimmed over his actual journey, mentioning police chases, a run in with an enraged turkey hunter, and a motel that burned to the ground during his brief stay. "I think it was some sort of trap to get me, or even kill me!"

Frankie B ended up in Kansas where he built himself "some pretty decent" living quarters in the third escape tunnel of an abandoned salt mine in Hutchinson. He had electricity from his portable, gasoline — powered generator and everything else he was able to purchase at the Hutchinson "Yeah, Come On In, We Might Have It or Something That Resembles It" grocery store in town. For expelling body waste—he used the fourth escape tunnel.

He said that he did part time work, home repairs, that sort of thing during the day, but at night, "I began to study the mind and saw how the brain has such magnificent capabilities and how I could use those locked powers and become the smartest man in the world!" All while eating a limited diet of Pork Rinds ("Lotsa Protein!"), Coffee and Hog Jowl and Pineapple pizza he actually had delivered to his "house."

"So," I interrupted, "How did you get to be the smartest man in Nebraska while living in Kansas?"

"Well," he replied, " I set up a program that measures my knowledge against different groups of people and/or animals, or regions of people and/or animals. When I first started, I immediately found out that I was only smarter than the 'Adobe Mud People' of some small island in the Pacific located only a few miles from where they conducted nuclear detonations or a group of semiconscious dolphins with sinus infections. But after time, I found myself getting smarter and smarter. Soon I was smarter than the average 12th grader in an alcohol rehab center or the state of Alabama. Now, I am smarter than an elderly chimpanzee in a narcotic test laboratory or ¾ of the population of the state of Nebraska! You have to start off step by step ya know!"

"What the…?" I asked very, very confused, "That's crazy talk! How the hell can you do that? How can you possibly…..?"

"Never mind," interjected Frankie B, "It is something so complicated, so horrendously intricate and sophisticated, it might make your head explode! So what are you working on? I can help you!"

A very large part of me was saying, "Don't ask! Please, for the Love of God, don't do it!" But it was the very small part of me, curious at the oddity that had presented itself, that wanted to see what would happen. Of course, nowadays, I no longer listen to that part. Well, not that much at least.

I glanced down at one of the articles from a women's magazine that was titled "Soon—To—Be Mammas Have the Greatest Dreams!" and blurted out to Frankie B, "So, what do you know about pregnant women and the dreams they have?"

Frankie B, started by taking a deep breath, then leaning forward with his elbows on the table said, "Young man, I'm glad you asked."

He leaned back into his chair and then proceeded in telling me a long and highly convoluted story that began with an encounter he had in a small Kansas Bar/Truck Stop with an ex—Army Private who was a "Pothead and an Alcoholic. I believe the proper scientific name is 'Weedboozer…' who played rhythm guitar in a "piss poor" garage band and used to be a kick boxer. He was, that is, until he, "Accidentally killed a 1750 pound heifer in a fit of drunken rage aimed at the Dairy Industry—he was lactose intolerant, you see. He was also smacked out of his mind on crack and some really cheap whiskey that even a dying dog wouldn't drink. The whole thing scarred him for life—it really did!"

The self—proclaimed "Smartest Man in Nebraska" continued on, managing to weave such an incomprehensible litany of verbiage which bounced back and forth across centuries and topics (he somehow managed to make a direct connection between the Egyptian Sun God, Ra and the surgeon who implanted the glass eye into the head of entertainer, Sammy Davis, Jr.). Had I actually tried to focus and try to understand what he was saying, I'm certain that I would have suffered irreversible damage to my brain, or, in the least, a raging migraine.

About 40 minutes later, in his only reference to the question I had asked, he mentioned that his mother—after consuming a spoiled chocolate glazed donut sometime during her pregnancy with his little sister, "Nicki B. You know, short for Nicole B."—had a dream about eating a giant marshmallow and when she awoke, her pillow was gone.

A joke. And a bad one at that! I sat there listening to this pompous windbag talk about things he had no idea about, make shit up, and just plain babble only to get a lousy joke. I got up from the table and leaned over to Frankie B.

"You're an ass!" I started in a harsh yet hushed tone, "No, wait! If you were smarter, then you'd be an ass! Maybe if you teamed up with that dope—smoking, guitar playing, kick—boxing, Army rejected booze hound, the both of you could equal the intelligence of a braying jackass waiting in line to have its head bashed in so they can make high school cafeteria food and a pair of work boots from it!"

"Did you know," piped in Frankie B, evidently not fazed at all at my verbal lashing, "that my father, Horace B, actually came up with the word 'jackass'? Yep, it happened when he fell down the stairs at the grain silo while carrying a very large, awkwardly shaped piece of Monterey Jack Cheese. You, see, he was reeling from the effects of grain dust. The

Nazis once experimented with a concentrated form of grain dust to be used in place of mustard gas, which was, by the way, invented by my uncle, Morton 'Jumbo' B—he was 6ft 10 and weighed 415lbs—when he dropped an all beef hot-dog covered in spicy brown mustard and relish into a barrel fire at a construction site. He almost called it 'Relish Mist' ya know?"

"Shut, your friggin' pie hole!" I shouted—well, a library "shout" (sort of like a really loud, raspy whisper)—as I got up and left Frankie B, the "Smartest Man in Nebraska", to continue to ramble on to himself. This researching stuff was proving to be a hassle.

As I walked out the massive doors of the library, I realized that I still had the article regarding pregnant women and the great dreams they had. Being that it was still incredibly hot outside, I returned to the main lobby of the library and found a seat. I looked around to be absolutely sure that the "Smartest Man in Nebraska" was nowhere to be seen then began reading the article.

It started out with all the wonderful fluff on how terrific it was to be an expectant mother and, yes, those incredible outbursts of wild mood swings are perfectly normal. Reading further, it mentioned that women who are pregnant tended to have more "vivid and detailed dream sequences" than those who were not in that condition. It went on with excerpts from medical professionals who claimed that there was no succinct reasoning for such. Some claimed it could be "emotional manifestations" due to the fairly numerous mood swings. One said it could be do to increased blood pressure and water retention. Another "doctor" said it could be the voice of the unborn child produced in picture form. Yeah, I'm sure.

I put the article down on the seat next to me and looked up just in time to see the library police trying to haul out Frankie B. He was trying to explain, with his hands behind his back and this big, burly security guard prodding him along, that he was in the process of completing further study into the human psyche and that this would put him seriously behind schedule. I turned the other way, so as to avoid any eye contact with him as he was briskly shoved along a path that had him pass nearly right in front of me.

As I turned, I spotted a pregnant woman sitting a little table. In front of her she had a pile of four or five, irregularly shaped books (I couldn't actually see what any of the titles were, but thought that they may be children's book due to their unusually bright colors and odd dimensions) and what was apparently her lunch. She was eating a hot-dog with chili. On the table was another hot-dog with relish on it. There was also a small jar of dill pickles. And a small container of ice cream. There was also a large bag of vinegar and salt flavored potato chips, a plastic container of chip dip, a jar of pickled jalapeno peppers, several deviled eggs, a tin of kippers, and several Twinkies. Under the table was an open bag of pork rinds, a few cartons of Chinese food and a pizza box with the lid opened revealing four slices missing. Just looking at that combination of food she had laid out for lunch was making me queasy. I couldn't even imagine trying to eat all that at one sitting…

Then it hit me! Pregnant women didn't have vivid and highly detailed dreams because of emotional outbursts, hormonal imbalances or from the blabbering, highly unintelligible monologues delivered by the unborn fetus. They had them because they ate enormous amounts of such varying and contrasting foods—or just plain ole junk—all at one sitting!! That had to be it!!

I then decided that I was going to do my own research. From scratch. I was going to eat a whole lot of weird combinations of food, go to sleep, and then write down my dreams. I can eat (a lot, too!). I can sleep. Sounded easy enough.

"I don't remember you ever telling me that!" shrieked my best friend, as if on the verge of hysteria, "You never friggin' told me!! Un-freaking-believable!!"

"Oh, shut the hell up already!" I snipped back.

On the way back from the library, my mind was reeling. I was thinking about what I needed to do to start my "research." I decided to try some "experimenting" that very evening. The first thing I decided to do when I got home was start a journal. I would record what I ate and then what dreams I had. The thought of the work involved in keeping a journal made me a bit queasy. But, nonetheless, I was excited at the thought of doing something "scientific" and was eager to get started.

I ran into my room to see if I could find something that I could use as a journal. I went through all the notebooks and three ring binders that I had from high school. I had just graduated, and had a big pile of the stuff crammed into the corner of my room. Most of the notebooks had every page defiled with cartoon characters, words to songs, ideas and actual (thoroughly incomplete) screenplays—I wanted to be a movie director—and massive amounts of doodling. And a page or two of notes from my classes.

After some further rummaging through the pile, I came across a pink, spiral bound, 80-page notebook that I would not have been caught dead with in school. It even had images of little butterflies on it. I guessed that it must have been in a pack of "bargain basement" notebooks that we usually ended up with as a part of our school supplies. That along with "deeply discounted" number 1/2 lead pencils (very large—like writing with a boiled bratwurst sausage) and "Cheap Stick" —the actual brand name—glue (the nozzle was perpetually clogged and if you tried to squeeze it too hard, would simply explode out the bottom), we were set for the school year!

In any event, I decided that this notebook would be sufficient—at least to begin with—for my purposes. I opened it up to the first page and wrote:

"THE COMPLETE CHRONICLES OF INVESTIGATIVE STUDY INTO THE EFFECTS OF INGESTED FOODSTUFFS ON THE TOTAL RELEASE OF IMAGINATIVE IMAGES IN ANIMATED, SEQUENTIAL

AND EXACTING DETAIL FROM THE SUBCONSCIOUS CAVERNS
OF THE HUMAN PSYCHE By Dashel X. Gabelli, Pioneer of Science."

Hot Damn! This was going to be great!! I turned to the next page and
at the very top put the heading "The Beginning—July 9, 1981" and
began my journal by writing about my encounter with Frankie B. After
a few pages, I ripped them out and threw them away. If I attempted to
complete the section regarding that kook from the library, I would have
no room left for my 'research results.' And, this was MY study anyway!!

That evening, for dinner, I had a big plate of sausage and peppers
smothered in onions, a small block of goat's milk cheese, half a pump-
kin pie, a cup of espresso and a slice of three-year-old fruitcake. That
should do it, I thought to myself as I went to bed. I kept thinking to
myself that I was going to have some really great dreams now!

The next day I awoke with a distended stomach and some cramps, but
no recollection of dreams. "Nothing happened," was recorded in my notebook for that day. And the next day. And the one after that. And again.

The day after that, I was able to record a somewhat fuzzy dream
involving Frankie B. He was standing with his hand up against a stone
wall (I didn't know where) talking to a really skinny blonde hair girl. I
couldn't make out much of anything for most of the conversation—just
murmuring sounds and the immediate surroundings were dark. Then I
was able to make out some of what he was saying.

"Yeah, you see," said Frankie B., "it's like this. I drew the pictures that
were on the matchbook cover and I sent them in, right? So I get this letter saying they were so impressed with my drawing of Mortimer the
Turtle and with my rendition of 'Close Cover Before Striking', that they
wanted me to enroll in their art school! And, get this! It's only gonna set
me back two maybe three grand at most! Impressed, huh?"

The skinny blonde was not. She just stood there, with some sort of
smoking device that looked like a metal tube with the coloring of an ordinary cigarette dangling from her lips and asked was there somewhere

they could score some pot. "And not that cheap, funky skunkweed crap you always want to smoke, you cheap-ass bastard!"

Frankie B, evidently ignoring her, continued on, "Hey, do you know what the difference is between an alligator and a crocodile? If you smack the beast with a broken off car antenna and it just up and snaps your arm off at the elbow–it's a crocodile. If it flips up and puts your head in it's vise-like jaws, it's an alligator!"

I could see the skinny blonde punching and slapping Frankie B. as the dream just faded into darkness. Well, I was able to put something in my notebook, though, to be honest, I was hoping for more.

The next night—nothing. Then again, nothing. Zilch the next night. I began to wonder if this was going to pan out at all. Me with my tolerance for patience hovering around zero was about to call it quits.

Then, just as I was about to toss this whole fantastic research "thing" out the freakin' window…

Section II

The Stuff Dreams Are Made Of

(Excerpts from THE COMPLETE CHRONICLES OF INVESTIGATIVE STUDY INTO THE EFFECTS OF INGESTED FOODSTUFFS ON THE TOTAL RELEASE OF IMAGINATIVE IMAGES IN ANIMATED, SEQUENTIAL AND EXACTING DETAIL FROM THE SUBCONSCIOUS CAVERNS OF THE HUMAN PSYCHE By Dashel X. Gabelli, Pioneer of Science.)

One particular evening I was at a party and in the typical way I tend to overindulge, I drank myself silly. Usually I don't get so inebriated when there is food available at a gathering, and I assumed that there would be since everyone knows I am a firm believer that eating massive amounts of food before consuming gallons of potent and unrefined alcoholic mixtures will soak up the toxic substance like some magnificent sponge and I'll be just fine—but the host of the party had only three hotdogs ("Chicken" dogs, actually—some "off–brand" made from chicken parts that were rejected by the dog food factory that sells a foodstuff concoction for mongrel dogs that suffer from no taste buds), an open tin of two week old anchovies and a package of Slim Jims from 1970 in the refrigerator. I had brought nothing with me to eat except for the little bag of stale potato chips I had laying in my car for three weeks. I left the party, after sobering up a bit, extremely hungry. I made the only decision one can make in a state of extreme hunger and semi-lucidness —I ate the rancid and dusty potato chips that were under my car seat (some had actually managed to stay whole in the crumpled foil wrapping). And I stopped by a fast food restaurant.

It was late and it appeared they were in the process of closing. Well, I assumed they were cleaning the place as I saw a young freckle—faced girl wearing a brown uniform spraying an extremely watered down and highly carbonated cola mixture on a young man apparently sleeping on the frying grill. Either that or he had been on fire prior to my arrival.

The young girl did not seem too happy to see me and made a great variety of faces and curious snorting and huffing noises from her mouth and nose that distinctly expressed her displeasure when I ordered. Needless to say, it took some time for me to receive my food, having to roll the smoldering boy off the grill and all.

I finally received my food—three of the 2 1/2 lb (weight AFTER cooking) Cheeseburgers, four orders of their famous "Bamboo Stalk" fries (the fries average 15 inches in length made from "Giant, Genetically Enhanced Siberian Potatoes") and a five liter Humongo Drink ("The Drink to Have if You've Mistakenly Ingested a 10lb Bag of Road Salt—Or Eaten One of Our Slick and Salty Burgers")—and went home. I ate the food in a matter of moments; when I'm drunk and hungry I eat a lot and very quickly. A group of radical, hippie college students (who managed to finagle a grant from the government by posing as a group of Middle Eastern geniuses who wished to develop a superior laundry detergent that would make clothes not only cleaner—but glow in the dark as well) at the University of West Virginia conducted an experiment where three Appalachian Mountain people (they did walk upright on two hind legs, but other than that, the "people" classification wears thin) drank a gallon of pure moonshine—the same stuff they use to blow out oil well fires—then proceeded to consume a 1400 pound heifer in fifteen minutes. I imagine it would have quite a bit taken longer had they made the effort to kill the beast and cook it.

I finished eating my purchase of grease and highly concentrated sodium products and guzzled down a gallon and a half of some sort of cheap, discount store brand fruit drink (that giant carbonated beverage that I purchased with my meal wasn't enough to re—hydrate my shriveling, screaming for fluids blood cells) that I had in my decrepit refrigerator that always freezes my eggs and leaks 40 gallons of water each day. Looking like the Michelin Tire man with a distended stomach, I stumbled to the sofa and fell into what I believed to be a coma. I then began to dream….

In the dream I was sitting on the dusty, brown ottoman watching the eleven o'clock news. The plain—looking female anchor was droning on (over video clips) about two lions that had been running loose in the city. Apparently the monkeys at the zoo staged a riot after being denied access to the same high grade feed pellets (with vitamin C and fluoride for clean animal teeth!) the lemurs were receiving. During the Level 6 lock down— the one right below calling the National Guard—an animal rights sympathizer released the lions, all the while singing, "Born Free" through one of those giant megaphones college cheerleaders use to scream words that sometimes rhyme and make no sense at football games. In gratitude, the two lions promptly shredded the activist like confetti.

The lions had spent the better part of the day chasing large dogs and small cars. Fortunately, the lions only caused minor damage—though the minister of the Church of Somebody Special had his Yugo battered and savagely mauled, causing nearly $35 in damages. Insurance adjusters have declared the automobile "totaled." The minister appears on the screen, nearly in tears, squeaking like a dog's chew toy, "I can't believe my car isn't worth 35 friggin' dollars! Though, I do have to face the facts, it really is a crappy car!"

After chasing a group of bio—mutated, genetically re—engineered, rabid dogs that escaped from the SPCA's "We Really Do Some Really Crazy Things In There" Research Center, one of the lions, apparently trying to catch his breath (probably not enough exercise at the zoo) inhaled a Chihuahua and it had become lodged sideways in his wind-pipe. While the one was slowly suffocating to death, trying to cough out the glob of canine clogging his airway, the other rushed at full speed towards a team of firefighters who were in training (trying to put out a fire that started when a group of flea—infested, drunken bums' wiener roast got out of control). The ferocious beast, perhaps liking it to a large African Boa Constrictor, bit into a fire hose that pumped nearly 4500 gallons of high—pressured water into the beast causing it to burst like a piñata, spewing fragments of flesh and bone of the animal known as "The King of the Beasts" for nearly a square city block.

The camera then switched to a distinguished looking gentleman who was going to deliver the evening's human-interest story...

"During the past year, an intensive market research study had been conducted and the results are in—Americans will not eat flavored shoe leather for breakfast. In a staggering defeat for the fast food chain, which was excited with the idea of being able to use every bit of the cow for edible products, a court order has banned the sale of such items as food. As you know, the company has had tremendous success in the recent past with their 'I See You' caramelized cow eyeballs and 'The Big Kiss' sugar—coated bovine lips. Even the cheap toys that are doled out with children's meals are manufactured from cow bones, adenoids, cartilage, and hair.

"The tests, done over vast demographic categories of the country, all indicated that the same cross section of the population that whole—heartedly embraced the most recent innovation–'Here's Licking at You, Kid,' the deep fried strips of cow tongue—thought the idea of flavored leathers to be a horrendous abomination. The major food chain had hoped to appeal to the younger generation, the ten to twenty year olds, with their Michael Jackson endorsed leather foods. The youngsters not only rejected the idea, it was met with outrage. In a letter written to the Attorney General of the United States, a Georgia teen thought that the person who came up with the scheme to push off what in a sense is a shoe with coloring, flavor enhancements, minuscule amounts of vitamins and virtually no minerals as a breakfast food should, quote, be shot, hung, tar and feathered and fed to hyenas. I ain't eating no friggin shoe for breakfast!, unquote.

"'We're surprised that today's youth with their unbridled enthusiasm and thirst for new things could think such horrible thoughts,' said Ronald McDonald, the spokes-buffoon for the famous food chain in part of a written statement released late last night. Mr. McDonald was the mastermind behind the leather breakfast biscuit, envisioning the idea would be a smashing success—on not only for the children, but for the entire family as well. Apparently, he was wrong."

(Ronald McDonald, who without that white make-up and orange wig looks a lot like John Belushi, is now on the screen smoking a cigarette and holding a glass of what appears to be scotch. He is squinting through the smoke and is slightly swaying back and forth in his chair, evidently inebriated.) "I figured that especially the kids, God love 'em, would, you know, fall for the whole gimmick. You know, Michael Jackson and all that crap. (Takes a long drag on his cigarette, the ash falling on his stained and torn Pink Floyd T-shirt) I figured the kids would go crazy over the stuff. I mean, look at the junk they eat in the morning now! Nothing but a damn bowl of sugar! Makes the kids go crazy! Jumping around like friggin' dirty animals...(takes a gulp of scotch, dripping out of the corner of his mouth onto his shirt). Leather ain't got no fuggin sugar! I'm just trying to be a humanitarian! I wanna help the little bastards!! Did you know that for everyone of these 'shoe foods' we sell, 12 1/2 cents goes towards my program to assist Children With Athletes Foot? I'm like friggin' Jerry Lewis here, raising money for these wonderful charities! Ah, screw it! I hope their teeth fall out of their friggin heads! Get that Goddamn camera out of my face! And, kids, don't forget that I'll be at the mall tomorrow to sign autographs and give out some cheap, probably disease—laden, crap manufactured with cow pieces! And Stay In School!"

"After speaking with several dietitians in the area, this reporter has found that shoe leather is not at all fit for human consumption. It simply doesn't supply the necessary nutrients in a balanced diet. Especially so for young, growing children. Uleedelbas Tard, a dietitian for the Public School System explains." (Uleedelbas, a 50-ish looking woman with her hair in a net and smoking a corncob pipe is on the screen).

"While it is true that if no other form of nutrition is available, shoes can be substituted for a minuscule amount of basic nutrients, but in no way can they actually help the body of any human being, let alone a growing child. Oh sure, there have been some documented cases where people who were stranded on deserted islands where no food whatsoever was available, have survived for two or three hours by chewing on leather like rabid, filthy dogs, but they died eventually. Human beings are not like goats. We can't survive by eating candy wrappers and barbed wire. What's next...chocolate covered battery casings? Mentholated rubber band candies? Vanilla pencil eraser pie? It's horrid! Why can't the children just eat the good food that God put here for them? Like chicken bologna. Now that is REAL food!"

"When asked what Mr. McDonald's punishment should be for suggesting such a hideous plan to sell un-nutritional and potentially dangerous food and direct it towards youth who are easily fooled by fads and just about anything else, Mrs. Tard replied and I quote, I personally think that the guy should be shot, hung, electrocuted, put through a wood chipper, burnt to a pile of ashes, spread over the desert, collected in a jar, mixed with water and lard, baked for three hours at 350 degrees, sliced into thin deli slices, be put back together and do the whole process over again for thirteen times, and after the last time should be fed to piranhas, who should be fed to sharks who in turn should be incinerated and the ashes should be mixed with cement and used as a foundation for building that would manufacture chicken bologna and those little teeny sausages made out of imitation lard and pork, end of quote.

"Mr. McDonald will be held in police custody, charged with conspiracy to undermine the general health of today's youth. Some think that Ronald McDonald is actually a member of the Chinese Intelligence Service and has been systematically implementing the much rumored 'Master Plan' to overpower the United States by creating fat and lazy children that will eventually have no will or desire to get off the couch and go outside as the Reds march down Main Street with their paper mache dragons doing that crazy Russian Dance where they jump and hop around. If this is the case, he will be shot.

"More on the fast food wars in the morning."

The news then went into commercial and I got up to change the channel. I inadvertently turned to a station that was showing an infomercial. It took a few seconds to realize it was for some new fangled exercise machine. Mr. T, still brandishing that stylish Mohawk and 80 pounds or so of gold jewelry, was trying to explain in his yelling kind of way that this new machine can stretch your spine and that in twelve weeks you could be foot or more taller. From what I was able to gather, this newly patented mechanical contraption utilizes high—torque hydraulics and galvanized steel, high—ratio gearing and what appeared to be simple bicycle chains to "gently and with only mild to moderate discomfort" stretch the lumbar region of your spine so you have a large torso.

They were showing before and after pictures and everyone looked like they were standing in front of fun house mirrors; small legs, humongous torso, little head. It looked like a carnie freak show. Some were giving testimonials on how happy they were, being a foot or more taller. More self-confidence, they were saying. People looking at them with respect.

I found that part hard to believe since they were all dressed in muumuus because they don't make clothes for such distorted body dimensions. One young lady, who looked absolutely ridiculous with her red and orange with little purple flowers muumuu, claimed that she was only 5' 4" a month ago. Now she was 6' 7". She was beaming with pride as she blabbed on about how thin she was now and able to go out and hold her head up high. She actually began crying and sobbing like a baby as she was thanking Mr. T for helping her to "see the light." "Get away from me, you crying fool!" screamed back the T Man, "Stand up like a man and face the world like a tall person!! That's pitiful!!"

All this for seventeen easy payments of $39.95! "I pity the fool who don't stretch their torso!" shouts Mr. T.

I then got up and switched the channel (evidently I can't find the remote even in my dreams) to another news station. They too had a fast breaking news story on the fast food industry. The female anchor, which looked like a cross between Cindy Crawford and Dr. Ruth, began her story...

"Burger King had expected to come out with their new line of imitation beef burgers, but a Federal Court judge thought otherwise. Judge Franklin Felonious, of the lower court circuit, today banned the new burger due to overwhelming evidence showing that the burger was unfit for human consumption. The federal agencies involved in pushing for the decision all agreed that such an item on the market would cause several hundred injuries, and possibly deaths, each day.

"Last year, The Magic Beef Man had proposed an idea of making a hamburger that would cost virtually nothing to produce and could be sold for far less than the average fast food hamburger. For years prior to the Magic Beef Man's suggestion the company had been losing millions in market share to their competition. Burger King scientists have been trying to develop a process of making cheap cuts of spoiled burro meat look and taste like they could be edible, but cost projections indicated that this would be prohibitive to the bottom line, being only a barely perceptible small step down from what they were already doing. After several months of new research, the scientists came up with a plan they thought would work.

"Behind the highly guarded doors of the heavily fortified 'Magic Mansion', where all research and development are conducted, the burger enterprise had developed an incredibly advanced and secret method of making shards of highly volatile sodium and fragments of rusted ship hulls smell and taste almost like beef. The process, which involves a molecular 'breakdown' of the basic compounds and then reassembling them into a new form, stretched the bounds of the imagination as well of known scientific theories. The newly concocted plan looked like a winner to the ailing fast food chain.

"While their creation may have tasted and smelled like beef, it certainly did not look like any beef available on earth. Even the nearly rotten jackass meat and meat by products forwarded to third world nations, who are accustomed to eating sand, beetles, and lizard crap, looked tastier. It came back from the kitchen absolutely hideous, colored black and purplish-green with yellow specks. The people responsible for the burger were hard at work trying to develop a new food dye that would make the their burger look less repulsive, yet be different than any other comparable product on the market.

"After four months of testing, a new type of dye was created. Plaid #399 made the hamburgers look like an argyle sock and the foundation for a marketing bonanza was laid. After getting Barney the Dinosaur to put his signature on an endorsement contract that would let Burger King name the product 'Barney's Super Dee Dooper Tasty Technicolor Burger', market research was done to determine if this new idea would fly. The fore polling proved to be promising with over 75% responding that they would welcome a change to the standard, old looking burgers at the fast food chains.

"Before actually putting their burger on the market, Burger King had to get the seal of approval from the Food and Drug Administration. At first sight, the highly respected members of the FDA testing team did not think anything out of the ordinary, just a cheap gimmick to get customers. There are no laws against this, but there are laws for attempting to kill people. Not only did the tests indicate that the food stuff was potentially deadly, with severe bouts of gastrointestinal discomfort and an incredible bloating on the cellular level causing the body's blood cells to burst like teeny water balloons as the 'minor' side effects, it also discovered that combining sodium with rusted metal proved to be explosive. While attempting to cook three of the experimental patties, a tremendous explosion rocked the FDA test kitchens in Washington, D.C. killing four FDA personnel and spewing a dense, malodorous cloud of toxic fumes, similar to the aroma and incredible internal pulmonary burning of lethal mustard gas or a typical Friday rush hour in Los Angeles, into the afternoon skies.

"It was also discovered that the food dye, Plaid #399, P399 for short, caused rapid bone disintegration in the hand. Several test monkeys lost all the bones in their hands after ingesting approximately one gram of the food dye. They also suffered unimaginable bouts of extreme halitosis, the stench being so noxious that several FDA team members began bleeding from their eyes before passing out and being sent to local hospitals. Another side effect of the dye was the severe drying and flaking off of three layers of skin around the ears. The FDA finally decided that enough was enough and they were not going to approve the burger.

"The Burger King people were astonished at the harsh decision handed down by the judge. Mr. Adolph Reginitis of the Burger King public relations department issued this statement. Quote, We really don't see anything wrong with our product. It's just that the government doesn't want us to overtake McDonalds, which everyone knows is run by the CIA. Everybody has food that can sometimes cause trouble—yes, occasionally even long and painful deaths. It is something we all deal with. We are not the only ones, you know, end of quote.

"Criminal charges have been brought against the Burger King hierarchy. The charges range from murder—of the four FDA testing team—to conspiracy to commit mass murders by selling their product to the unsuspecting public. The charges have been filed with the Criminal Supreme Court this morning, and all counts combined could put those involved away for 227 years. Since they could be eligible for parole with good behavior in 102 years and prosecutors don't want them to ever get out, they will be pushing for the death penalty."

(Assistant District Attorney, Geraldo Heltzenfeld—who looks a lot like Joe Pesci—is now on the screen) "Personally, I would like to see them skewered on big sticks and roasted to a crisp over a big bonfire. Anyone who even considers doing what these jackasses wanted to do should at least, at least mind you, be publicly tortured. Death would be too good for this bunch of scumbags. I wouldn't mind personally beating the hell out of them with an aluminum softball bat then chopping them into small pieces and feeding them to the lions and elephants in the zoo—if they would even eat that crap!"

"Burger King personnel have been ordered to keep quite about the 'minor incident', even to their own families. Burger Kings in three of the lesser populated states and in Puerto Rico will be closed for fifteen minutes on Thursday after the lunch crowd leaves so the problem can be ironed out, stated Burger King officials. Now it's time for the live lottery drawing!"

The screen then went to the live drawing for the $316.5 billion dollar lottery jackpot. The lotto machine seemed to stretch on for what appeared to be the length of a football field. It seems that they draw 217 numbers and a Super Ball. In order to win the jackpot, you must have all 217 numbers in the exact order they were drawn, the Super Ball number and the ticket must be the shade of blue that they choose for that drawing. If you manage to get 216 numbers in the exact order they were drawn, the Power Ball number and the correct shade of blue ticket, you win a Mr. Freezy artificially flavored onion Popsicle and a mildly tattered and soiled "Take This Job and Shove It!" T-shirt.

They mentioned that no one has won the lottery since 1921, and that person suffered a fatal heart attack upon finding out she won. They also showed a picture of a balding, overweight man with a Popsicle in one hand, wearing the prize T-shirt—which appeared to be several sizes too small for the gentleman—and a frown on his face. He was the only winner of the "consolation" prize, awarded in 1967. The jackpot has been rolling over since.

Well, I certainly wasn't going to sit there and wait for them to draw 217 numbers and a Super Ball, so I got up and shut the TV off. Just as I did the power went out in the house and I had to stumble about into the kitchen with the last match I had burning itself down to my fingers to try and find the only candle I had. A big '3' from the cake at my third birthday party. I located it in the infamous "junk drawer"—right in the middle of 47 dead AAA batteries, three toenail clippers, four miniature golf pencils, an open package of geranium seeds, scattered thumb tacks and paper clips, and the keys to my 1972 Pinto that blew up in 1979 when a dog catching a Frisbee ran into the back bumper—and managed to light it off the gas stove.

I then glanced out the window to see Gilligan mowing my lawn on a riding mower made out of palm leaves. He was trying to smoke one of those two-foot long Three Stooges cigars. After the dreadfully thin Gilligan took one long inhale, he developed a pained look on his face as if perhaps he were suffering from some severe damage internally and crumpled to the ground. I imagined the same look would come across my face if I attempted to inhale a bowling ball through a coffee stirrer.

Thurston Howell III and Lovey were following behind collecting grass clippings and listening to the stock market report on that crappy white radio they had. When they saw Gilligan collapse to the ground, they turned to see if anyone was looking then began rifling through his pockets. All they found was a lousy lucky rabbits foot. "Not very lucky today are ya, punk," squealed Lovey. I then awoke to the alarm clock blaring "Daydream Believer–The Hyper Dance Mix" and promptly ran to the bathroom and vomited.

Later in the day, I was amazed as to the detail in which my dream appeared. In my notebook I noted, "I am now more than anxious to continue my dream study!! Let's bring it on! Hot Damn!! I think this research stuff is really going to wreck my stomach and maybe some other organs!"

✶ ✶

In the quest of further dream research, I went out and ate a huge bucket (67 Pieces! Including Our Famous "Grilled Gizzards!") of greasy fried chicken and coleslaw (yes, the coleslaw was greasy, too) and consumed a few alcoholic drinks—my infamous mint juleps made out of grain alcohol and Scope Minty mouthwash. I went to sleep that night with my stomach churning and my head spinning and pounding like a jackhammer. After several "close calls," the waves of nausea passed and soon I was in dreamland.

In this dream I was still living in my parents home, sitting in a big black chair in my room looking at my collection of what I thought were my books from childhood. But the titles were a little unusual. There was *James and the Giant Pomegranate* right next to *Charlie and the Munitions and Chemical Weapons Factory*. There was my collection of Curious George Books: *Curious George Robs a Bank, Curious George Goes to the Betty Ford Clinic, Curious George Splits the Atom, Curious George Gets Indicted for Mail Fraud, Curious George Beats A Small Dog With a Golf Club,* and *Curious George Gets His Ass Kicked by the Man in the Yellow Hat*. And right there next to my hardback edition of *The Catcher in the Pumpernickel* was the *Big Book of Mother Moose Stories*. I took it down off the shelf and opened it up. It was wonderful! Big, vividly colored drawings that seemed to jump right off the page!

I started reading some of the short little ditties that Mother Moose was noted for. "Jack be Nimble, Jack be quick, Jack got third degree burns on his ass jumping over an alcohol flame…you big Dunce!," "Hey, diddle, diddle! The cat and the fiddle, The cow jump-started my car; The little hamster laughed to see such sport, And the egg ran away with the thermometer," and "Little Jack Horner Sat in the corner, Eating a scalding hot Christmas Pie: He put in his thumb, And pulled it out screaming, And said, 'What a complete ass am I.'"

I then turned to further on in the huge volume where the longer stories were. Then something magical happened. All the drawings were moving like animated characters! It was amazing! Then a voice came from the book (sounded a lot like Orson Welles with some minor nasal congestion) that said, "Relax as I regale to you a tale." This is gonna be cool, I thought. It was like watching a cartoon movie!

"Once upon a time, on a little farm far away, lived three slightly large hogs. They were happy and content as all sloppy, lazy, filthy animals should be. Occasionally, the three of them would romp around the surrounding countryside, playing games and waxing philosophic. They truly had the happy life….until….

"One day, the pigeon who lived atop the silo came flying into the barnyard, shrieking at the top of its little lungs. It appeared that there was danger. The pigeon was so excited that it couldn't speak, just shriek like some crazy, hysterical lunatic whose medication had worn off and straightjacket was on too tight. One of the hogs, Eugene, grabbed the pigeon by its scrawny little neck and began to throttle it in an attempt to calm the frightened bird. After a few minutes of this, the pigeon was dead. Now they would never know what the danger was, they surmised. So the three of the hogs gathered around, skinned and cooked the bird in a rosemary and red wine marinade and had a delectable appetizer.

"The next day, tired of the foul smelling stench they had created in their own home, the three little hogs decided to go out and get some fresh air. They ran around the giant trees, played hide and seek, king of the hill, leap frog, dodge ball and Australian Rules football until they were nearly exhausted. They then stumbled across some tracks in the dirt that they had never seen before. They sat around and had an open discussion as to whom or what the tracks belonged to. After eliminating a few dozen or so animals (they for a brief moment considered the tracks to be made by a blue whale), they narrowed the possibilities down to two: the scarce, two-horned, black rhino—or a common wolf. This must be what the pigeon was squawking about, they agreed. They then went back to the disgusting, dung covered, rat-infested barnyard they called 'home'.

"Three days later, they again ventured into the woods forgetting all about the tracks they had found earlier. They once again ran about playing their games when they noticed a small cottage off the main path. Intrigued, they headed towards the structure wondering what was in it. Before they could reach the cottage, a giant, overly obese wolf wearing a tattered, smelly Boxcar Willie outfit and large, multi-colored bowling shoes appeared in front of them.

" ' Hold it right there!' thundered the huge creature. ' Where do you think you are going?'

" 'Well,' answered Cecil, the biggest of the three, 'if it's any of your damn business, you freak, we're just roaming around getting fresh air, soaking up the rays, nothing in particular.'

" 'Oh yeah?!' bellowed the obese wolf while swatting at the swarm of flies circling his head. 'It's been three days since I've last eaten and I am extremely hungry. I believe that I will eat all three of you for my supper!'

" 'All three of us?' questioned Milo.

" 'Yes, all three of you!' replied the Wolf.

" 'Well,' piped up Milo, who sounded a lot like a slightly more mascu-line Richard Simmons, 'that's an awful lot of saturated fat and choles-terol you're thinking about ingesting and by the look of you, I think that wouldn't be a wise decision. As a matter of fact, I believe that you could afford to skip a few more meals and perhaps begin a regiment of exercise and a low -fat diet. Did you know that Little Bo Peep used to weigh 345 pounds! Now look at her! She really has it going on! She simply followed my fantastic 'Feed Your Face' meal program and got some exercise. Let me get my boom box and we can start with some low-impact aerobics right now!'

"Well, this inane suggestion infuriated the beast who let out a tremendous, but wheezy roar and began chasing—if one can call hobbling and weaving like a staggering drunk with arthritic knees chasing—the three hogs throughout the woodlands. Eventually all three of the snorting hogs ended up at the cottage before the wolf could get them. As if that blob of bones could ever run faster than 1 mph. They were peering out the window when they spotted the wolf near a tree trying to catch his breath and mumbling something about now being a real good time to quit smoking 3 packs of unfiltered Camels a day.

" 'Wow, this guy is never gonna catch us! Just look at him!' chuckled Eugene, 'I've seen healthier horses in line at the glue and hot-dog factory!'

"Don't be too surprised," said Cecil.

" 'Yeah, don't forget the story about the three little pigs. They thought they were on easy street early on, too,' warned Milo.

" 'What are you, drunk or something? Did you get into Farmer Johan's sour mash again? Were you inhaling aerosol fumes or 'huffing' gasoline this morning while the rest of us were eating our slop? Did you find some of those 'wacko' mushrooms growing in our shit again? Or are you just stupid? Look, those were little pigs and everybody knows that hogs are much brighter than pigs,' stated Eugene with an air of confidence.

"All of a sudden the wolf was pounding on the front door with fervor, the tremors shaking the frail cottage. 'Let me in you stupid little hogs or I'll huff and I'll puff and I'll blow this teeny little pile of scrap particleboard held together with nothing more than spit, shit and rusty thumbtacks to hell and back!'

"The three hogs showed no outward signs of fear, sitting down on the sofa and rocking chair watching the last quarter of a football game on TV and scarfing down boxes of stale cereal, beef bullion cubes and pancake mix they found in the cupboards.

" 'Ah, go kill yourself!' shouted Eugene with his mouth nearly full of shredded wheat and rice puffs smothered in a whipped, pseudo–cheese formulation from a dented can.

" 'Alright! That does it! I've had it up to hear with you brazen beasts and now you're gonna get it!' screamed the wolf. 'I'm gonna huff and I'm gonna puff and I'm gonna blow this God-forsaken cottage into the wind!!'

"The behemoth took three steps back and stared intensely at the cottage. He took a deep breath, tightened his belt (if you can call a decrepit, frayed piece of rope a belt), counted to three, then he huffed…and he puffed…and he suffered a fatal heart attack, crumpling to the ground in a tremendous heap of flabby flesh, matted fur, colorful and stained hobo clothes and really cool looking bowling shoes.

"The three hogs came running out of the cottage to see what had happened. When they saw the huge mass of the filthy, god—awful smelling animal on the ground they all began to sing 'Who's Afraid of The Big Bad Wolf.' When they got to the third verse, the ground started trembling under their feet. They clung to each other, unable to move, frozen in terror. They managed to turn around and see charging towards them a massive, 3500 lb, scarce, two-horned, black rhino. Before they could utter a word, they were trampled to death, mangled beyond recognition.

"Moral: Don't push your luck."

Cool story! At this point in my dream I was about to turn the page and looked forward to be entertained with another fable when the phone rang. I picked it up and said hello but received no response. Then out of nowhere, the Queen of England was on the other end. She was asking if I was able to come over to the castle and have some exquisitely prepared smoked pheasant sandwiches and brie. I declined reminding her that was what we had last week and unless she can come up with something new, not to bother me. I also mentioned that I believe I had lost a leaky, disposable pen at the castle and thought that perhaps it was in the sofa somewhere and would she mind looking for it. I put down the phone and it immediately rang again.

I let it ring a few times thinking that I had perhaps offended the monarch and she was calling to chastise me. Then I thought that maybe she had found my chewed—on, cracked plastic pen and I picked up the receiver but on the other end wasn't the Queen of England. It was a woman who was offering to have phone sex with me if I ordered her new book on adultery and sewing machine repair. I politely explained that her other book on bondage and do-it-yourself refractive laser eye surgery was presently being used as a platform to hold an old, leaky car battery. I then slammed the phone down at which point I woke up to the alarm clock ringing.

* * * * * * * * *

During my one year of college, I stuffed myself with all types of junk food to avoid eating the cuisine specifically engineered to gum up the intestinal tract they served in the dining hall three times a day. After I was asked to leave school (some little misunderstanding about prostitution, grand theft, extortion, kidnapping, racketeering and assault and battery—quite silly actually), I was sick of eating junk food, but deathly afraid of eating "regular" food. This caused some degree of difficulty when I was invited to people's homes for dinner. Everyone would be dining on superbly prepared meals and I would crunch on anisette toast—the wonderful Italian cookie designed to keep beaver teeth from getting too long. I still liked to eat pizza and whenever I did it would bring back memories from my college days.

One night during my freshman year (my only year), myself and several acquaintances (other academically floundering and often inebriated students who lived on the same floor of the dormitory) attended a seminar on how to buy property with no money down. Being that we were college students with no money, this sounded like something we could do. Well after fifteen minutes of wonderful testimonials given by once destitute people (one gentleman was actually living in a kettle drum at the opera house!) who have managed to rise above the ruin and utter humiliation to purchase millions of dollars of real estate, own private jets, yachts, Rolls Royce automobiles and now hobnob with the beautiful people, we came to the unanimous conclusion that this was a crock of shit.

We left to go to the local pizza joint where we proceeded to polish off seven pitchers of beer and five pizzas (there were only three of us—well, in reality there were 5, but two couldn't eat nor drink since they had their jaws wired shut after a college prank involving chewing gum, rice krispies, hydrogen peroxide, red wine vinegar and gunpowder went slightly awry). In our severely bloated state, we somehow managed to return to the dorm, our bellies so drastically distended that I still have stretch marks to this day. With my digestive system on the verge of simply shutting down due to being so completely overwhelmed, I returned to my dorm room, stumbled on a pile of discarded cigarette cartons and old Rolling Stone magazines, smacked my head against the air conditioner, collapsed to the floor and was asleep in minutes. Then the dreaming began…

In this particular dream, I am lying on the bed in my dorm room watching television. After channel surfing (which meant standing at the TV and turning the dial with a set of pliers, being I had somehow lost the actual dial) for a few seconds, I stopped on PBS. I never watch PBS unless they are having a Monty Python marathon, Benny Hill is on, or they have that really cool white guy with the afro and laid back speech pattern painting pictures, but for some reason I stayed there.

I was just catching the tail end of a promo for a PBS Grand Slam Wrestling Match. Mr. Snufalupagus and Big Bird were teaming up go against Shari Lewis and Lambchop in a no holds barred death match. "I'm gonna stuff that sock puppet freak down that friggin' witch's throat!" shouted Big Bird. "There's gonna be meat on the street—Sesame Street that is!" screams the annoying Lambchop. Grover was trying to separate the two sides, but Mr. Snufalupagus swung his trunk and smacked Grover's head off. Cool, I thought. The melee fades to black and in really cool, red neon graphics pops up: "This Ain't Yo Momma's Public Television!"

The screen gets all fuzzy and squiggly (cable wasn't mainstream yet) and I get up to readjust the coat hanger draped with aluminum foil that still had bits of a grilled sandwich stuck to it. The picture then comes back nice and clear. It took a couple of seconds to realize that they are now showing a televised seminar, similar to the one I had attended earlier that evening about buying things with no money.

The gentleman who was giving the seminar looked like a young and dynamic person with exceptionally large white teeth that would give any individual the right to believe that either this person's mother or father was a horse. I thought to myself, now here is a guy who could use a couple of boxes of anisette toast to keep those choppers in check! He was impeccably dressed in a dark blue three-piece suit, white shirt and red power tie. He seemed to exude confidence except for the fact that he was squirming around like he had to pee. He removed his jacket to reveal large sweat stains under each arm as he briefly stated that tonight he would be talking about opportunities available to college students to make significant amounts of money while still in school. It sounded interesting enough. Then his left eye began to twitch uncontrollably and he started speaking in a booming voice, sounding like a cross between James Earl Jones and Pee Wee Herman...

"Did you know that most young adults upon graduating from high school go right into college? Well, it's true! Instead of going right into the work force and becoming responsible and productive members of society, they want to LEARN MORE to possibly EARN MORE by getting higher paying jobs! They HAVE to EARN MORE because they now have to PAY for having gone to college! It's a vicious circle that keeps college graduates deeply in debt with nowhere to turn. Let me elaborate. (He walks over to a stool set up on the stage, his shoes making a sound like a pet's squeaky chew toy. When he sat down it sounded like, though I'm not positive, he farted.)

"People have always asked why anyone would put up so much money to further their education. The answer of course, is quite simple; they don't. The typical college student relies heavily upon subsidized state and federal loans and/or parents to foot the bill. In the case of student loans, the student, not being the brightest bulb in the house (or why would they be in college?), takes the loan and figures that since he or she is going to college, he or she will get that high paying position they always dreamed of and immediately pay off the loan. This is the number one, biggest mistake.

"An individual who graduates from college will realize that in the four years he or she was in school all those wonderful, high paying positions have evaporated into thin air. He or she then gets a job hauling garbage, pumping gas, agreeing to be a guinea pig for highly dangerous biomedical research projects or cleaning out filthy animal cages. Of course, this is only temporary. For this, they wasted four very precious years of their lives? And in the case of relying upon parents, who at that moment in their lives are not looking forward to a major financial burden, the results can be absolutely ruinous! Take for example, the story of Mr. and Mrs. Hubbard and their daughter Rebecca of Odessa, Texas. (On a huge screen behind the speaker a picture of the Hubbard family appears. A striking, middle aged man with thick wavy hair, a beautiful blonde hair wife and a stunning, blue-eyed, blonde daughter are standing in front of a very nice looking two-story colonial house. As the speaker stands, he knocks over the stool.)

"The Hubbard family was the typical, mid to upper middle class suburban family. B. Jack Hubbard was the lead head basher down at the slaughterhouse and earned a fairly decent income. Jocelyn Hubbard was a typical suburban housewife who supplemented the household income by selling macaroon art, piñatas stuffed with egg salad and frozen beef Popsicles door to door. Rebecca was the Hubbard's only child and was quite spoiled by her parents. Rebecca did well in school, but not good enough to get a scholarship to any college. But she needed to go to realize her dream of becoming a meteorologist and taking the place of Dancin' Debbie Dustbowl, the local channel 23 weather girl who danced around practically naked while she talked about fronts, lows, highs and hellacious hailstorms. (On the huge screen appears Dancin' Debbie Dustbowl wearing fishnet stockings, a g-string and cumulus cloud formation pasties…almost made me want to move to Texas).

"Now, B. Jack didn't see the sense in sending his daughter to college. He had done just fine for himself, thank you very much, without anything more than a fourth grade education (On the big screen is a picture of a smiling B. Jack Hubbard wearing a bloody white coat, hip wader black boots and a sledge hammer in his hands standing in front of hanging cattle carcasses), and really wanted his daughter to come work at the slaughterhouse as the 'gut -ripper-out girl'—a very coveted position! Each year, there is a calendar featuring the 12 most beautiful 'gut-ripper-out girls' in the state of Texas (On the screen appears the calendar with Miss March, Patti Sue Williams of Austin, wearing a black thong bikini bottom and a white, half T-shirt—which barely covered her ample bosom—that had 'EAT MEat' printed in bold, red letters across it. Patti Sue was holding a large clump of tripe in her left hand and a cow lung in the other. She had a big smile on her face that showed her pearly white teeth.) B. Jack thought that his daughter would surely be one of them if she would only come to work with him. But Rebecca wanted to go to college.

"Rebecca, who was known throughout the county to be an incessant nag and chronic whiner, put her foot down and demanded that she go to college. Well, her father, who had always given into his daughter's demands, reluctantly agreed. But how was he going to pay for it? Sure, B. Jack had some money, but sending Rebecca to school would wipe out anything they had saved for retirement. Then B. Jack had an idea.

"B. Jack decided that he would invest a little money and throw an old fashioned fair in his backyard to raise money to send the spoiled beyond recognition Rebecca to college. He rented some ponies for the kids, set up some midway booths, hired some carnival freaks and leased a giant Ferris wheel. Everything seemed a little cramped in the small backyard (Picture on screen of the Hubbard backyard looking like a fairground—with rows of games and attractions—only about 100 times smaller), but B. Jack anticipated a huge turn out. He was right!

"People from miles around saw the giant Ferris wheel looming into the suburban Odessa sky and came to join in the festivities. There were hundreds of people there, each spending their hard earned money to see the freaks, ride the ponies, and blow a weeks paycheck on the rigged carnival games to try to win stuffed 'things' that, if you were delirious with a high grade fever, resembled animals. B. Jack was proud of himself. He was going to make his little girl happy. Quite a few people were milling around the giant Ferris wheel anxious for a ride. When there were 175 or so people demanding a ride on the giant wheel, B. Jack decided to turn it on.

"B. Jack, not being the smartest person in the world with a fourth grade education, didn't realize that you just can't plug a tremendous piece of motorized machinery like a Ferris wheel into an ordinary electrical socket, which is exactly what he had done. Expecting to amaze the crowd with the flashing lights and loud carnival music that usually emanates from these attractions, he flipped the on switch. The smell of electrified air filled the neighborhood and the hair on the back of people's necks stood straight up. The gargantuan circus ride had sucked every last bit of electricity out of the Hubbard house and caused brown outs in a large pockets across the county.

"Inside the Hubbard household, the refrigerator imploded to the size of a toaster oven...the microwave's door blew off and the super-energized microwaves reduced the dinette set to smoldering kindling. The family's pets, Ollie, the cat and Midge, the German Shepherd came running out the back door looking hideously freakish without a hair on their bodies (On the screen appears a picture of the two pets, completely hairless and with bulging eyes). And B. Jack's most prized possession, the 52" 'Magna Theater' television system with state of the art, highly advanced audio reproduction, was vaporized. And to make matters worse, the crowd was getting restless, demanding to ride the Ferris wheel.

"Well, when B. Jack announced that the wheel would not be operational, the crowd went hysterical! They starting turning over booths and lighting fires. Then the huge mass—in one tremendous effort of human strength—toppled the gigantic carnival ride on to the once lovely Hubbard home. (On the huge screen is the mangled steel wheel sitting atop of what looks like a pile of rubble with people throwing partially filled popcorn bags, waffle cones, chili corn dogs, and stuffed 'things' on top of it). The crowd then got completely out of control spilling out into the once quite suburban neighborhood, turning over cars, smashing mailboxes, and relieving themselves in neighbors' bushes and lawns. The police in all their riot gear and hauling the 'Block Buster' water cannon appeared on the scene in an attempt to restore the peace (On the screen is a picture of police in full riot gear and Billy clubs raised charging into the crowds. The 'Block Buster' shooting high-pressured water into the melee knocking people off their feet. Small clouds of tear gas can be seen wafting over the heads of the mob. Pretty neat.)

"The police managed to bring order to the situation and the crowd eventually dispersed. No one was really hurt beyond a few cuts and scrapes...well one of the freaks got kicked in the face by a terrified rabid pony…but that only added to his drawing power. But poor B. Jack Hubbard! His home a shambles! All his savings and then some going to pay for this debacle. He managed to settle the class action lawsuit out of court by agreeing to sell the rights of his horror story to the plaintiffs. He was now a truly broken man…all because Rebecca had to go to college. He decided to send her to a convent instead. Now look at the once proud Hubbard family (On the screen is a picture of a man and a woman who look exactly like Ma and Pa Kettle alongside a sullen looking girl in a nun's habit standing in front of what looks like a garage at a public storage facility in downtown Odessa). Makes me sick just looking at them. (The speaker turns his back to the audience—who see the split in his trousers—and retches onto the floor. He turns back around and wipes his mouth with his shirt sleeve).

"Now, while the Hubbard's situation is certainly not common place, the threat of a tremendous financial burden is. So, if someone must go to college, what can they do? How can they help ease that load? How can they pay their ENTIRE way through school? The answer is for the individual going to college to make as much money as possible while they are IN school. How can one possibly do that? Well, pay attention, as this information I am about to bestow upon you will change your miserable, pathetic little lives.

"First of all, forget all about those typical part-time jobs. Those will only provide you with 'chump change' that you and either your boyfriend or girlfriend can spend at Pop's Malt Shoppe. Or spend it all on pot or blow it all on a hooker—and a cheap one at that! It will not even put a minuscule dent in that tremendous financial burden you have created for yourself. Did you ever hear of the phrases, ' A drop in the bucket,' or, ' A spit in the ocean?' Keep those in mind when you get that job at the local burger joint flipping frozen, preformed meat by product patties in that really snazzy brown uniform or when you're asking your clientele whether they prefer paper or plastic or when you're the chump of the day cleaning up the spill in aisle 7.

"The only way for you to truly get ahead is to make money unethically and perhaps slightly illegally. Of course, you must not get caught because we all know that hauling garbage is much more fun than rotting away in a cramped, stuffy cell at the state penitentiary where your cell mate is a convicted ax murderer who threatens to cut your fucking head off each and every night and you have to sleep with one eye open and you develop chronic bleeding ulcers from the incredible stress—or so I've been told! (The speaker has sweat flowing down his face that he wipes with his jacket he picks up off the floor. The sweat stains under his arm are barely noticeable now that his entire shirt is drenched.)

"So how does one develop inside them the ability to do something they are not normally accustomed to doing? How does one live outside their, quote, comfort zone? Because if you are planning to really make money while you're in college, you're going to have to change your mindset. This is the single most important thing you have to do and is the key to the entire program being realized. And this is how you do that…"

At this point they break away to one of those extremely annoying pledge breaks they have on PBS, which they seem to have nearly every other week. It always has amazed me how they come on and beg for money when they are receiving billions of dollars in grant money from the CHUBB group, whoever the hell they are. The guy is telling me how if I want to continue to see top quality programming like the seminar I am watching, I need to send some money in.

They were, however, offering some neat tokens of appreciation. If I pledged $700, I could receive a Bert and Ernie ashtray and solar—powered opium/hashish water pipe kit that actually talked to you every time you lit up. "This is one of the most absolutely fascinating smoking devices I have ever seen!" the guy running the pledge break said, "You have to got to hear this thing!" He then pressed a small black button on the side of Ernie's head and it begins to talk in the voice of the characters.

"Hey, Bert…Bert…Can you hear me, Bert buddy?" asked the Ernie side of the smoking 'thing'.

"Ernie, I'm right here next to you. How can I NOT hear you? I hear you all the freaking time!" replied the Bert side.

"Oh yeah, you're right, Bert. Hey Bert...Bert...Hey Bert!"

"WHAT! What is it, Ernie? You're driving me out of my freakin' mind!" replied the Bert side.

"How about a song, Bert?"

"Oh good Lord, no! Please, Ernie, no more singing! You really don't have a good voice and you might scare away the person smoking!"

"Rubber Ducky, you're the one," Ernie begins singing, " That brings me so much fun..."

"Oh God!" mutters Bert, "Not that crappy song again! Please, somebody kill me. Just pull me aside, put a gun to my freakin' head and put an end to my miserable existence! Please!"

The gentleman then turned off the contraption with tears running down his face since he was laughing so hard. He then proceeded to go down the list of other items available to the viewers for their contributions.

If I pledged $1000 I would have the opportunity to get a Masterpiece Theater lunch box with the image of William Shakespeare on the outside and a recreation of the balcony scene from Romeo and Juliet printed on the thermos inside (autographed, of course, by Alistair Cooke) or a set of Mr. Roger's brass knuckles. The pledge guy assured the television audience at home that these are the same ones Mr. Rogers used on that little king puppet on an upcoming episode. They even had his initials engraved in them as well as small particles of the fabric that the little puppet king is made of stuck into the slightly jagged edges! It also comes with a certificate of authenticity framed for anyone to proudly display in his or her home.

After a few minutes of rattling off names of individuals who had actually pledged something, and running down some other things they were offering —a Boston Pops screwdriver kit, a Sesame Street do-it-yourself pap smear test and a Mcneil-Laher News hour gasoline siphoning tube among them—they returned to the seminar I so wanted to see. It returned "in progress," so I missed the all-important thing I needed to know to get out of my comfort zone. I was pissed! The speaker looked a mess. He had somehow lost his pants and was standing there in a soaking with sweat, stained shirt and tie, ratty and frayed green boxer shorts, pink socks and brown loafers. He was pacing back and forth, eye twitching and shoes squeaking, nearly shouting as he was addressing the audience…

"…they will be so freaking grateful, they will adopt you, or give you some outrageous cash reward! And if they don't—take 'em to court, suing them for faulty security or endangering a human in their home or something! I'm sure with all those blood-sucking pieces of wild animal fecal matter called attorneys out there, one will show you the right path to take! Then, go out and find some other wealthy family to invade! Can you see…can you comprehend…is it soaking into those fucking pieces of granite you call heads, how incredibly easy this all is! It's as easy as taking a piss! (At this point you can see liquid streaming down his leg and wetness spreading over the front of his ratty boxers. He stands in the puddle and raises his arms as if to silence the audience, but no one is making a sound).

"Now, I've just given you just a few suggestions on how to make life at college just a little bit richer—or a whole lot of hell richer if you stick with it, if you know what I mean! (Evidently no one did, as there was total silence)…Now it's up to all of you out there to come up with something and put it to your own use as soon as possible! If all goes right, you should be able to pay off those loans and retire at 24! If you fuck it up, get a good lawyer and remember—you didn't hear it from me!"

He now outstretches his arms and lets his head fall to his chest. A moment of silence, then a tremendous thunder of applause. People screaming, women crying tears of joy…some jumping up and down in their seats…roses were being thrown at the stage…security guards came out to prevent the horde of screaming fans (remember the Beatles at Shea Stadium?) from rushing the stage. He lifted his head and smiled.

He turned to walk off stage, but slipped in the urine, sweat and vomit combination on the floor, landing flat on his back, where he remained while the credits began rolling. The applause, cheers and screaming didn't let up at all during the entire list of producers, lighting technicians and such that scrolled on the screen.

The screen then cut back to that annoying pledge break where they mentioned if I gave them $14,000 they would send me a boxed edition of the speaker's video seminars. They included: *How to Scam First Graders Out of Their Recess Candy Money, Run Your Own Floating Crap Game the Fifth Grade, Loan Sharks—A Nasty Name for Some Mighty Fine People* and *How to Hypnotize the Bank President Into Giving you Millions*! Wow! I thought, some pretty neat stuff.

Then the jackass down the hall was pounding on the door shouting in a drunken stupor asking if I could help him rip the pay phone off the wall because it kept telling him that his girlfriend's number had been disconnected. I got up and opened the door to find him slumped down on the cold tile floor. Oh well, I thought, closed the door and went back to see what was next on the tube.

I sat back down to see Julia Child running around with her hair on fire yelling, "My hair is on fire! My hair is on fire! For the love of God, somebody help me because my hair is on fire!" Evidently she put too much cooking sherry in the soufflé (and down her gullet, as well) and blew up the kitchen. She ran off camera as the credits began to roll and the set turned into a raging inferno. Off camera I could hear the obnoxious lady shrieking "Jesus Christ, can't you see that I am on fire? What's the matter with you assholes?! Put me the fuck out!!" I then heard what sounded like a fist hitting a face and loud thump as if a humongous sack of cement hit the floor. Then my roommate stumbled in, a complete drunken mess, laughing about how stinking drunk he was and needed some air. He went to the window, opened it, and stuck out his head. Then he just fell out!! I awoke in a cold sweat on the floor and glanced over to see if my roommate was there. He was lying with his head on the floor and his feet up on his bed. I was tempted to wake him and tell him about my dream, or at least get him to get his whole body into bed, but I let him sleep that way and couldn't wait to watch him try to explain why half his face looked all puckered from being pressed into the carpet.

*   *   *   *   *   *   *   *

Since my revolt against the homemade Italian cooking that I was accustomed to–"The Great Upheaval" as I like to refer to it—in the fall of 1983, I have always been on a quest to challenge my somewhat desensitized palate. In the never ending search for unique tastes and the dreams that accompany such "new" meals, bizarre sandwiches have become a specialty of mine. The combinations of different ingredients you can use are thoroughly mind-boggling! You can mix anything together and throw it on two pieces of bread, a hoagie roll or even some stale, moldy, saltine type crackers, and voila—a bizarre sandwich!

The main idea here is to combine things that you would not normally eat together in one bite in your lifetime to create highly unusual, foreign tastes and, of course, cause metabolic reactions that will trigger your brain into releasing certain specific and otherwise dormant biochemical extracts into your body that will cause you to have vivid and sometimes horrifying dreams. It really is a lot of fun!

For instance, not too long ago, late at night, I wanted to get something to eat before I went to sleep. I couldn't figure out exactly what I wanted, so I pondered a few moments and decided that I would surely love a bologna sandwich. Hot Dogs and Bologna have always been favorites of mine, not only because they taste so damn good, but because I never really knew exactly what they were made of. And I never really wanted to know. It added a touch of "mystery" to my meals. As I savored every bite, I would imagine that they were perhaps manufactured with baboon nostrils, zebra gums, or weasel tendons. Something exciting about eating wild animals, even though I did know that they were made from various parts of domestic farm animals—though I wasn't sure which parts.

Well, anyways, I looked, but there wasn't a miserable slice of bologna in the whole house. Not even under the sofa cushions…yes I looked. When you can't find something that you want to eat, you become acutely aware of your hunger and have to have something to eat immediately or you will absolutely die within a matter of moments. So I went to work to see what was available for me to eat.

I rummaged through the kitchen, the crawl space under the house and the garage and found two slices of seeded rye bread, mustard, ketchup, a can of tuna (from a time when they were still allowed to catch and grind up dolphins and whales), and some old spaghetti sauce (again, from a time they could grind up dolphins and whales). I figured, what the hell, and threw them all together into a "Sandwich of the Damned" (it wasn't really that bad—I refer to all my unique creations as such. "Salad of the Damned," "Meatloaf of the Damned," "Artificially Flavored Fruit Drink of the Damned" and "Dashel's Dental Cleansing Solution of the Damned" are just a few of my favorites).

I ate the whole magnificent creation in about 27 seconds and washed it down with a gallon and a half of Elmo Gantry's Amazing Synthetic Water. With nearly everything I ingest requiring some taste and texture to it, real water wasn't good enough for me. Sure, it was a little crazy to buy water, but with all the un-dissolved minerals, gel-like suspended solids, some rather large microorganisms, and heavy metals in it, it was actually cheaper than tap water per pound. I went to bed happy that I had finally found something to eat—and would not die of hunger in my sleep—and went off to dreamland.

In this dream, I was at the dentist's office, sitting in a chair wondering what exactly I was doing there being that my teeth felt fine. The lady sitting next to me, however, appeared to have something wrong. Her cheeks were puffed out like someone had shoved a couple of billiard balls in her head. She looked a lot like Louis Armstrong when he's blowing that freakin trumpet so hard you think his veins are going to burst and drench the audience with spouting blood. Across from me was an elderly gentleman who looked fine...until he yawned and his mouth opened up so big that one could shove a basketball in there—except that a few seconds later, his bottom jaw fell to the linoleum floor. This is strange, I thought to myself.

I also noticed that patients were being called from the waiting room into the back office, but that no one was returning! This peaked my anxiety a bit, being that I am already terrified of going the dentist. I decided to take my mind off of my fear by reading a magazine. I looked down at the coffee table in the waiting room and just grabbed the first magazine I saw—a Highlights for Children. I started leafing through the rag—I've always enjoyed a good Highlight—picking out all the cool stuff.

Goofus and Gallant was always a favorite of mine. It was a good indicator on how well you were being raised. As long as you didn't behave or look like that filthy, ignorant, punk monkey Goofus, you were being raised properly—even if you didn't always act like that squeaky clean, pussy whipped, tight-ass Momma's boy, Gallant. I quickly found the Goofus and Gallant section and thought it look a bit peculiar. The first panel has Goofus with his back towards the reader with his pants around his ankles, his ass bared. In front of him was a group of people staring wide-eyed, mouths agape. The writing below the picture: Goofus doesn't wait until he is alone before he begins masturbating. Opposite was the Gallant frame. It showed Gallant with a look of terror on his face, mouth wide open, fumbling with some little canister with his hands. The words: Gallant doesn't masturbate. He holds in all his young preteen, raging hormone driven, sexual tension until he develops asthma, suffers from occasional seizures and experiences periodic blackouts.

The next panel showed Goofus with a shovel out in the back yard with a cat, hair standing straight up, clinging to his head. The words:

Goofus doesn't wait until his pet is dead before burying it. The Gallant picture showed a massive funeral scene with limousines and a hearse and hundreds of mourners. The words: Gallant rants and raves until his parents take out a second mortgage on the house to spend $137,000 to have his hamster mummified and placed in a specially sealed and temperature controlled glass exhibition case at a pet mausoleum.

I turned back a few pages and saw one of those cute poems that they have in that publication. The picture was that of a little girl lying in a hospital bed with tubes and hoses running from her body:

"My stomach gurgles,
My esophagus burns,
My gums are bleeding,
You'd think I'd learn,
From my intestinal cramping,
To the fire in my spleen,
That young children,
Shouldn't siphon gasoline"

I flipped ahead a few pages and saw one of those pseudo-news articles that magazines use to appease their big advertisers. They attempt to make a newsworthy story out of some lame product or event. Never saw one of these in a Highlight before, I thought to myself. I decided to read on.

It's That Time of year Again!

CRAZYASSCO PRODUCTIONS of Pennsylvania, Inc. is holding their annual "Do Anything Just as Long as it's Crazy Ass Strange" celebration this week. Activities will be too numerous to mention all, but we'll try to shove as much as we can into our publication since our client has threatened to take his business over to Humpty Dumpty magazine unless we start pulling in some business for him. As many of our readers will recall, the previous celebrations were all smashing successes! All the favorites will be back again this year, plus some new attractions and those ever popular (and sometimes explosive!) surprises!

Returning again this year is the tremendously exciting Crazy Ass Zoo for the children and adults who can't sense danger. All those who visit this attraction will have the opportunity to touch and feel assorted wild beasts from the jungles of Africa and other places afar. Super, genetically enhanced mutations of every vicious species will also be on display at the Petting Safari! Children and child—like adults alike can truly enjoy themselves as they frolic with and tease the starving animals that were savagely beaten and terrorized with electric cattle prods before being released into the crowds. Who can forget last year when little Billy James got his foot lodged in the windpipe of a super sized, savage, Hungarian tree weasel? And all the time spent trying to get the young Agnes McGillicutty's head out of the ass of the monstrous, Australian scream-ing hippopotamus? You just can't forget times like that!! And please, no flash photography as it tends to spook the already half—crazed animals!!

That favorite showman of children and adults alike will be returning again this year!! After last year's slight mishap—where after removing his magic, collapsible lung, he carelessly tossed it into the Den of the Damned filled with highly venomous Devil Snakes—Bombardo the Clown has again agreed to make an appearance and perform his famous magic tricks and hand out highly toxic, hydrogen balloons and unfiltered Mexican cigarettes to all the children. Bombardo, who is best know for his tricks of swallowing three pounds of red, African clay, then shitting a brick and pulling out his lower lip, placing a huge watermelon in there and asking the children to smack him in the head with a 25lb sledge hammer, is suffering from some slight brain damage due to the massive amount of Devil Snake venom that had coursed through his veins. It's a miracle he's even alive!! Come see what crazy things this jackass will do this year!! Please, use your flash bulbs at his shows!! The bursts of light will cause him to slip into various stages of dementia!!

Another favorite event will also be back this year!! Capture the flag using small caliber firearms will take place on Sunday afternoon after all the wild, starving animals have been beaten one last time and sent out into the 14,000 acre park. This has always been a spectacular event!! Last year over 17,000 participated!! Two massive armies, all packing heat, in search of the other teams flag!! Can you feel the excitement!! Well you should!! If you can survive being shot at, being mauled by famished and insane beasts, avoid land mines and assorted booby traps—including, but not limited to—bear traps, spike pits, trip line activated bamboo spears, and those nooses on the ground that grab your foot and fling you into the air like a slingshot, you must grab the flag from a machine gun protected bunker!!

Remember last year, when Sister Elizabeth Flanagan managed to grab the flag, with most of her team either hanging from trees or from the mouths of enraged, wild animals, only to slip in a pile of moose dung fracturing her hip and discharging her snub nosed revolver into her thigh?! Needless to say, there was plenty of laughing as the red faced nun was carted off to the Crazy Ass Field Hospital where they poked her with stainless steel acupuncture needles, waved dead chickens over her head, rolled her around for an hour in a deep cleansing mud and put leeches on her to bleed the bad "demons" causing her pain.

A new attraction this year will be the Nero Night Competition. At this crazy event, Christians will be forced to face professional gladiators and mangy, LSD injected lions. All those who manage to survive the first round, move on to the big prize round!! Each will be handed a fiddle. Every custom designed violin contains an internal combustion system that causes the instrument to burst into an inferno of flames by simply dragging the bow over the strings once!! The actual contest is to see who can hold onto the blazing fiddles (which are continuously spewing out fire balls like a Roman candle) the longest!! The winner wins a carton of homogenized and pasteurized 2% fat milk (those teeny cartons–the ones even smaller than they give you in school). The losers all will receive consolation prizes ranging from travel sewing kits to pairs of 46" bootlaces!! All participants will receive a home version of the game to play when they get drunk and /or stoned with their friends!

And who can forget the food?! You certainly won't!! Chefs and short order cooks from restaurants long closed by boards of health and high-security penitentiaries from all over the world will be competing for the judges' taste buds! These highly talented and deranged artists will be delving into their own secret cookbooks to bring out their best weapons in the Battle of the Foods!!

Last year's champion, Juan Luis Jesus de La Merde Smith, will be back trying to hold on to the cheap, bent, aluminum soup ladle glued to a piece of scrap wood with rusty, tetanus bearing nails sticking out that we call a trophy. Mr. Smith won with his famous "Go to Hell, You Gringo Bastard" chili. Who can forget the look on the face of one of the judges when, after sampling Mr. Smith's crazy concoction, his feet swelled to three times their normal size rupturing his designer Italian loafers like a defective spleen?! I'm sure that particular judge will never forget!! A short visit with the leeches at the Field hospital had him in proper work-ing order in no time, although he did lose a good portion of his small intestine and can no longer speak due to severe larynx damage.

Samples of the foods will be available for everyone to enjoy!! Prices for small snacks—bits of burro lips sprinkled with poppy seeds on a saltine, shredded ostrich neck on a crouton—are a mere three dollars and six thousand cents. Larger, meal sized entrees will also be modestly priced. For instance, a rack of whale blubber sautéed with onions and shark teeth, smothered in octopus suction cups will run an amazingly low two dollars and seventy-five million cents!! A whole, rotisserie roasted African Bull elephant with 7 French fries, 2 baked beans and a milk crate sized crouton, is only one dollar and six cents!!!

A wide variety of beverages will also be available to those who can drink liquids. The drinks themselves will only cost 25 cents!! The only added charges are for the cups and if you would some ice to cool down the scalding sodas and boiling, spoiled fruit juices. Cups are available for about 30 dollars each (Please, don't even think about bringing in your own cup. We have a detention center/concentration camp filled with scofflaws who tried to do just that. There is nothing like 6 to 8 weeks of hauling large animal dung in wheelbarrows with flat tires and bent axles in 90 plus degree heat to discourage such blatant disregard for the nearly invisible, fine printed rules and regulations—on the part of the ticket that easily smears with the slightest moisture—in the future). You may try to use the same cup over and over again—if you can. Our cups are made from the finest onionskin paper and are highly absorbent. A block of ice—the smallest available size weighs in at 3 tons—will cost about 95 cents.

Admission to this marvelous event is priced so you can bring the whole family. Children under the age of 20 are free!! Adults 21—23 1/2 pay 3 dollars!! Adults 23 1/2 and one minute—55 pay 3 dollars and one cent!! All those over 55 pay $45. Plenty of free parking is available at McCreedy's Automobile and Small Truck Destruction Center and Assorted Scrap and Melted Down Stuff Emporium located 17 miles from the park. A shuttle bus (the kind they use in India that holds roughly 413 human beings laying on top of one another) will make the trek over some of the roughest terrain in the world to bring you to paradise!!

This year's event will definitely be a grand event!! So, please, for the love of God, come out and spend some money!! We can't afford to lose this client!! If we lose this account, Highlights will have to become a porn rag, and you'll be reading that Humpty Dumpty piece of crap while you're waiting to get a big ass needle stuck into your butt or waiting to get those teeth yanked out of your mouth by a dentist who will stand on your head and use giant, rusty pliers. Please, have pity on our lame ass children's magazine. Thank you for your support!! Oh God, it's all over!

I was about to turn to the lady next to me with the humongous cheeks and ask her if she had read this, but she wasn't there. Neither was the old man without his bottom jaw. As a matter of fact, except for me, the waiting room was empty. I looked back into the back office area, but all the lights were out and I didn't see anyone! I decided that they must have closed and left me here. I was just about to leave when I heard a television set in what seemed a side office. I opened the door and saw the dentist passed out on the floor with a couple of tanks of nitrous oxide by his side. The TV was on and what appeared to be an episode of the Brady Bunch was playing.

In this particular scene the kids and the parents were sitting around that enormous dining room table. They were arguing about who had the best part in the school play when Greg tossed a salad fork at Jan that bounced off her head and stuck into the fleshy part of Bobby's upper arm. Mr. Brady screams, "Shut the hell up you goddamn kids!! Acting like a bunch of fuckin' animals!!" Mrs. Brady shouts back, "Mike!! They're our children!!" "Oh no, Carol," shouts Mr. Brady, " those three yellow-hair witches are NOT mine!!" All the time the kids are screaming, Mr. and Mrs. Brady are shouting at each other at the top of their lungs .

Alice walks in wearing a black silk teddy and gives one of her famous fingers—in—the mouth whistles. "Hey, do you mind?! I've got some business going on here!!" Sam the butcher enters wearing nothing but a pair of gold glitter Speedos muttering, "God, what the hell am I doing? My life really sucks. Selling shitty bits of tainted meat and gristle and now screwing with this…this…thing! Somebody kill me!"

The kids are now acting like rabid dogs, spit and partially chewed bits of Alice's really dry meatloaf spewing out their mouths, turning over chairs, pulling each others hair, punching each other, dishes and food flying all over the room. Mrs. Brady is just repeatedly slapping Mr. Brady whose face is bleeding. Alice has Sam in a headlock ramming his balding skull into the wall. Oh my God, I'm thinking to myself, I never saw this cool episode before! Just then the dentist stands up and asks if I would like him to pull all my teeth. I politely decline and turn to walk out the door when he hits me in the head with an empty tank of nitrous oxide. I immediately wake up and my head is throbbing!! Good Lord, I think to myself, now I see why they no longer grind up dolphins and whale and put them into tuna and tomato sauces!!!

*   *   *   *   *   *   *   *

For months I was trying all different types and combinations of bizarre sandwiches, always eating late at night and having quite memorable, though always not exceptionally detailed or long dreams. I once dreamt I was a spectator at a major golf tournament. I was just sitting there on this old, ratty lawn chair watching all these people jumping up and down because Arnold Palmer was about to tee off on the 14th hole—187 3/4 yard, par 3. I heard someone say that this was Palmer's favorite hole, having shot a hole in one 5 times. As he was about to tee off, I stood up and joined the horde of people watching him swing. As everyone was watching him swing, I was looking to the other side of the green at some girl who looked familiar. I couldn't recall who she was and turned to watch Arnie swing. I turned just in time to get smacked in the head with a speeding golf ball right between the eyes, slipping into unconsciousness.

The next thing I recall, I'm coming to in the medical tent (located by the lovely dog-leg 17th—545 yd, par 5, 3 sand traps and lovely tree lined water hazard). I see Arnold Palmer smiling at me. He starts telling me that thanks to me he made his 6th hole in one. Evidently my forehead corrected his slice, knocking the ball into the cup. For this he won a new Cadillac and a $50,000 bonus. He shook my hand and, in appreciation, gave me a carton of Russian cigarettes (made from feed corn, mud, and flavored with spoiled anise stalks) and a spike from an old pair of golf shoes he never wears anymore and left. The medic on hand said that's what he does every year. It's his favorite hole because the angle from the spectator area to the hole is perfect for him. Every year he smacks some-one in the head hoping for the hole in one. What a bastard—and a cheap one at that—I thought to myself. I then woke up. Not much to that one, I thought.

Another one along the lines of blurry details and not much in length (though is was memorable) came after I tried a bizarre sandwich with extra, extra spicy brown mustard topping the combination of high sodium and fat luncheon meats and runny eggs contained in the nearly moldy roll. In this one, I am about 8 or 9 years old and was in our wood paneled living room. I was dressed as a cub scout and there were other children as well (maybe 15 or so) dressed the same. I was assuming that this was a den meeting.

My mother was a den mother for our group of scouts, but she rarely did anything. That was my father's area. My mother would just cook 5–7 pounds of pasta (which the kids would devour) while my father had to try and come up with some sort of Cub Scout related game or activity. Usually something to do with Indians–making brown paper bag tents and stuff like that. This looked a little bit different than a typ-ical den meeting.

First of all, it appeared that all the parents of the scouts were also in attendance–a highly rare occurrence. I did notice next to the door that there was a large amount of camping gear (backpacks, tents, coolers, etc) and thought, well, we must be going camping. All the parents were milling around drinking alcoholic beverages and us kids were just kind of walking around doing nothing. Then I went into the "extra" living room that we had and saw a piano and a microphone stand. I was about to turn and ask my folks what all this was when all the adults came pouring in to the room. My father came up to the microphone and made an announcement.

"Well," he began in his heavily accented English, "tomorrow, she is going to be a very big day! I can't believe we are going to be walking around to make it to the top of the world!"

All the adults began cheering and whistling while us kids just looked at each other, none having a clue as to what was transpiring. My father continued.

"We are so glad to have Kay, from across the next door, to sing a song for us! And her husband, he is going to play the piano thing."

Everybody knew that Kay Steffano who lived next door simply loved to sing. However, she wasn't very good. But as the adults became more inebriated, she must have sounded better since she was always managing to sing at nearly every event that had all the parents. We usually went to play with legos or Tonka trucks or something. This time we stuck around as she wobbled and weaved her way to the microphone and her husband stumbling to the piano bench.

"This is for all you little, wonderful scouts who are going on an amazing trip tomorrow," she started, "You all know I sing, and I made up this little ditty. Now, it's going to sound familiar, because I stole the music from the Carpenters–On Top of The World."

Everyone began clapping–because she was going to sing or because she stole the music from the Carpenters, I didn't know. But her husband started the music and it sounded exactly like On Top of The World. And when she started singing, it sounded like Karen Carpenter. Except for the words.

"It's hard to believe what were about to do
Haul our kids and bags up to the tip of K2
Now, between you and I
We might freeze or we might die
It's really hard to tell 'til we get there

"You tell me that the Sherpas don't look bright
I look at them and I think that you're right
But don't say it out loud

Or they'll leave us in the clouds
To freeze like human Popsicles in dry ice

"We're on top of the world and at this elevation
You know we need canned air just to breathe right
Where's that dog with the booze in the keg strapped 'round his neck
I think we're trapped at the top of the world

"It gets so freakin' cold when comes the night
I think I've lost some bones and skin to frostbite
Keep on your gloves and your hat, your parka and backpack
So you'll look real good when then find you deep in the snow

"Gee, I m getting tired being up here
What's this? Good Lord! I think I lost an ear
Feel how hard the wind blows, crap; there goes all my toes
Will somebody please come and try to get me down

"We're on top of the world and I've lost all sensation
I think that my feet will have to just come off
This idea was fun next time just whip me with a gun
Somebody get me off the top of the world!"

Everybody (the adults) were clapping and yelling as Kay took a bow
and fell over. Her husband laughed so hard his toupee fell off and he
landed on his ass on the floor. The kids were looking at each other with
puzzled faces.

"What's K2?" asked Slaggy Joiner (his real name was Vince, but he
wore hand me downs and his pants were always baggy. His father called
him "slacky"–we called him Slaggy)

"I think it's the highest mountain in the world," I replied, "and I think
we're going to be climbing it tomorrow!"

Some of the kids started crying. I was going to ask my Dad if this was true when out of nowhere, Cher came up to me and kissed me smack on the lips. All of sudden I wasn't 8 or 9 but 29–30. I kissed her back when my freakin' alarm clock went off. Dammit!

      *   *   *   *   *   *   *   *   *   *

Sometime later I was having a somewhat difficult time falling asleep. I began to wonder if all this dream research and eating these crazy sandwiches, junk food and assorted goodies loaded with God knows what, was worth it all. I looked at my Kmart LED alarm clock. It showed 2:36 am. Well, since I always set my alarm clock ahead in an effort to never be late, I had to try to calculate exactly what time it was. I couldn't recall how far ahead I set the clock and spent a few moments asking myself why the hell do I have a clock if I can't figure out something as simple as what time it was. I then began to drift off to sleep.

In this dream, I was sitting in the guidance counselor's office in high school. Everyone in school liked to come see the guidance counselor because he had the new super computer which could tell from your grades and other information, like your shoe size, how many cavities you have, and if you were able to perform minor human oddities like twitching your ears or licking the tip of your nose with your outstretched tongue, what your best career path was. I was sitting in the outer office with some other kid while some girl was in with the counselor. You could hear everything that was being said, and for some reason that caused me to be concerned, fearing that anyone and everyone could hear what I would be saying to the him—which I had no idea what that would be.

I heard the counselor mumble something about that in just a few seconds we will have your life planned for you, or something to that effect. I strained to hear a little better and heard the girl say that she couldn't wait to see what she would be doing for the rest of her life. The counselor says something along the lines of about how lucky the students at this school were to have him and his super computer and that it is never wrong. Again the girl says that she can't wait. She began rambling a bit giddily on how she had told all her friends and her parents that she was going to discover what her future would be. She said that her parents were thoroughly convinced that the computer could only provide her with the best possible career choices, having read a detailed article about such devices in Almost Science magazine. Suddenly, I was able to hear the conversation more clearly.

"Ah…Here we are," says the counselor as I heard the sound of paper being torn off a printer.

"Oh goody," says the girl, "I really can't wait to see what I am going to be!"

"Okay, you've said that like about 50 times already. Relax, 'kay? Let's see. Okay, here it is. Well, Anabella, according to the infallible super computer which was designed by the most magnificent, super scientific minds on earth with programming assistance by yours truly, thank you very much, we have narrowed your career down to two possibilities," said the counselor.

"Okay, so tell me already!" says Anabella, just a little bit too excited, I thought to myself.

"Okay, well, the first choice, though not necessarily the best for you, is that of a biochemical research engineer employed by a major pharmaceutical firm or possibly the defense industry in the research and development of biological defense projects involving psychotropic drugs and nerve gasses," said the counselor.

"Wow! That sounds terrific! I've always loved science and finding out about things! I have always been so interested on how the human mind reacts to being manipulated and how I might be able to eradicate the human race as well! That is so cool! That computer is so amazing! My parents were right, that thing gives the best choices!" said Anabella, obviously happy at that particular option that was chosen for her. "What's the other one the super computer picked for me?" asked Anabella with a lilting emphasis on super computer.

"Okay, the next choice…" said the counselor, with a pause for dramatic effect, "…. is a rodeo clown. You'd be employed by a regional rodeo outfit and your primary responsibility will be to distract raging bulls—that have been taunted, teased and beaten—from goring to death the cowboys who ride for the best time to win money. You will also be responsible to entertain the children and adults in the audience by running around and acting like a damn fool. You will also be required to sit down and try to play poker in the middle of the arena while a bull that has smacked his head one too many times against the arena walls indiscriminately begins tossing you and your fellow clowns around like rag dolls. You may also be required to clean up after the filthy animals take a dump. Oh yeah, and you will drive a beat -up pick up truck with the outline of a naked woman in chrome on the mud flaps and a decal of the confederate flag on the rear windshield."

"WHAT!" shrieked Anabella, "A RODEO CLOWN?!? There must be a horrible mistake!"

"Oh, there's no mistake, Anabella. And with that grade point average of yours…uh, let's see…a 3.998, I believe…yes, 3.998, this is the best career choice for you according to the super computer. And we all know that the computer is never wrong," stated the counselor.

There was silence and the sound of a chair sliding on the terrazzo floor. Anabella walks out of the office with a dazed look on her face. "Good luck in the rodeo, clown," says the kid in the outer office with me, laughing, " maybe I'll see you at the county fair in between the polka band and REO Speedwagon performances. And you better damn well entertain me!"

Anabella just burst into tears and ran out of the office slamming the door behind her. "Whatta dope," chuckled the kid in the office. He got up and went into the counselor's office. I was thinking about how the hell could a computer, that had been so highly touted as this one supposedly was, make such crazy, non—correlating career choices. While pondering the possibilities of how something this ludicrous could happen, I missed some of the conversation between the counselor and the kid. I picked it up in midstream.

"Well, Tom, since YOU don't have a problem with the choices given you by the super computer, what can I do for you today?"

"Well, Mr. Bolten, it's kinda of a personal problem," said Tom.

"Well, lay it on me, kiddo. Let me see what I can do."

"Well, okay," he tried to lower his voice, probably knowing that I would be able to hear him in the outer office. "As you can tell, I am not that tall. Heck, I'm just plain old short! It bothers me that everybody else in my class is taller than me. It really hurts when they call me a 'shrimpo', 'teeny', a "midget', and a 'small ass motherfucker.' "

"Tom, Tommy, Tom man, come on now," said the counselor in a pleasant tone. I could feel the smile on his face. "You shouldn't worry about little things like that...oops sorry...I mean, things like that. When I was your age there were kids who I knew very well that weren't that tall who had incredible growth spurts the following year or two. I wouldn't worry too much about it."

"So, are you saying you were you this short when you were my age?" asked Tom.

"Oh, good lord, no! I wasn't a circus freak—looking midget like you! Not even close!" scoffed Mr. Bolten, "As if...I had broken pencils that were bigger than you!"

I heard the chair fall over and see Tom running out of the office with a mean look on his face. He storms out and I'm thinking this Bolten character is a real asshole! I'm also thinking that Tom is probably setting up a sniper position on the water tower across the street from the school. I get up and decide to leave when I hear Mr. Bolten call my name to come into his office. I poke my head in and tell him that I really have to be somewhere else.

"Oh, so you think you can come here and waste my time, Mr. Gabelli?"

"What? I haven't wasted any of your time, Mr. Bolten, and I do really need to be somewhere else."

"Yes, you do. You need to be in detention," he says as he holds up a pink slip in the air for me to take to the detention room.

Crap! I grab the slip and head out of the office. I hear him calling behind me, "Are you sure you don't want me to tell you what to do with the rest of your miserable life? I am quite good at it, you know." I muttered something under my breath like, yeah, probably like a worker on the assembly line that manufacturers those nifty sticks with metal points on the end that the convicted drunk drivers use on Saturdays to pick up garbage from the sides of the roads as part of their sentence, and headed down the hall towards detention.

I get to the classroom where detention is being held and I give the pink detention slip to the teacher. He barely looks up from his book he is reading and nods his head. There is only one other person in the room, and she was napping. So I took a seat near the TV set by the window and sat down and opened up a book. The teacher then got up, announced in a loud voice that we better keep it down in here or he will come back and kick us around the room like soccer balls, and left the class. After about ten minutes of flipping through some textbook, I decided the teacher must have went home or fell asleep on the toilet reading his book. I decided to turn the TV on.

I started turning the dial, but all I got was a snowy screen. I finally found a UHF station that came in real clear—which was plain ole crazy since the television had no antennae nor lots of aluminum foil or any variety of loose wiring running from the set to the window, which was the recommended proper accouterments in order to receive any type of decent reception from such stations. It was about 3:10 in the afternoon and a cartoon program was playing on the channel. Rocky and Bullwinkle to be specific. I had always liked that show. I caught the tail end of an episode, with the narrator spouting, "Is this the end of our hero? Or...Will the Evil Soul of Bullwinkle Come Back and Beat the Shit Out of Rocket J. Squirrel After Getting it on With Natasha?" It then went into a commercial for a collection of records with everyone's favorite commercial jingles on them.

I didn't recognize any of them except the Oscar Meyer Wiener jingle. I wasn't even familiar with the products associated with the jingles. There was one for some foot odor-eradicating device that was real peppy.

"Everybody with a nose knows that that unpleasant,
Sickening stench is coming from your toes,
So for the sake of your family and friends,
Don't use them, use those...
And those boats you call feet will
Always smell like a rose..."

A very sweet female voice was singing it as in yellow highlight was the name of the product "Sweet Sweet Sweat Killers". I didn't catch much of the rest of the commercial as the girl in the room with me began snoring, distracting me. I did manage to catch the end where you could send a check or money order for $19.95 to get 7 albums or $21.50 for two 8-track tapes. The girl in the room stopped snoring as her head came crashing down onto the desk with a heavy thud. She still kept on sleeping or knocked herself unconscious.

When the show came back from commercial, it was time for one of my favorite parts—Fractured Fairy Tales. I've always enjoyed the crude animation and narration of this cartoon feature and was looking forward to seeing it. I only hoped that the teacher would still be on the crapper or had actually gone home.

The beginning animation for the segment came on and the narration along with full cartoon color came to life on the school TV.

(Imagine the cartoon characters moving along to the narration)

"Once upon a time, in a place far away, lived an ugly, dyed redhead girl who happened to be the princess of Borington. Her father was the king, her mother, the queen. They all had one thing in common, besides being related—they were all extremely bored.

"Dammit, I'm bored," muttered the king.

"So are we," screeched the princess and the queen simultaneously.

"You see, Borington was the epitome of boredom. There was absolutely nothing to do except work. Oh, sure, for entertainment, there was an old, decrepit magician, Carumbo, the Much Misunderstood Stupid One; whose only trick was pulling rotting possum carcasses out of an oversized pencil sharpener, but he was mainly there for the tourists, (one accidentally stopped by three years ago when his scooter hit a pebble in the road and blew out both tires), since the novelty had long gone stale for the people of Borington. And since there was no organized sports and no television or radio or even an Elks club, the people had nothing better to do than watch their crops of multi-colored flax weed—used in the manufacture of…well, we don't really know—grow.

"This sucks," said a group of 7 or 8 peasants in a monotonous unison.

"Now, since royalty doesn't work, the king, queen, and princess truly had nothing to do. Oh, sometimes they would ride around in the royal coach—an AMC Gremlin, with the engine removed, pulled by 113 mangy, flea—bitten cats and a 22 year old kangaroo with a truss on—to check on the crop of multi-colored flax weed and make inane suggestions to the peasants."

"Please, don't defecate in your pants when you get frightened," said the king.

"Please, please, oh kind and gentle peasants, keep your shoe laces tied or you might fall and split your head like a watermelon," chimed in the queen.

"But there was only so much of that they could do before the peasants would get pissed and threaten to kill the royal family."

"Shut the fuck up, or we'll kill you," said the same group of 7 or 8 peasants in monotone unison.

"They were all depressed, especially the princess. The King and Queen noticed how despondent the princess was and how much uglier she was becoming as well. They agreed that they had to do something or she would become the most ugly boring person in the world. She was eighteen and had absolutely nothing to look forward to. All she ever said was ' I'm bored to death,' over and over."

"I'm bored to death. I'm bored to death. I'm bored to death," said the princess.

"We know. Shut up already," said the King.

"The King and Queen got together with the Minister of Finance and discussed the possibility of sending their daughter on a short vacation somewhere. They themselves had never taken vacations, except for their honeymoon to Orlando, Florida. And that was only because they answered an ad for a timeshare that they received in the mail, addressed to 'Occupants'. They never would've been able to afford it otherwise and they were thoroughly excited at receiving the little globe compass that sits on your dashboard for sitting through a high-pressure sales pitch. As much as they loved the place, they just couldn't afford to do much of anything. The King, when he was a prince, lived in Borington and had no money and the Queen, when she was a princess, lived in Quailsvilla and had no money. When they married and merged the kingdoms into The Unified Federal Republic of Borington -by—the—Horrendous Salt Flat Wastelands (Borington for short), they still had no money.

"Now, about 19 years later, they have managed to save some of money from the multi-colored flax weed harvest (evidently, a small group of mentally deranged radicals have found that by mixing the multi-colored flax weed with marijuana increased the value of the pot. It also made the eyes of the user bulge out really far, which, of course, is funny whether you're stoned or not) and could afford to send their ugly child somewhere. They thought that a ski trip to the Alps would be wonderful. Since Borington is flat as paper, she would love the mountains.

"They told the princess and she was happy to be getting away from the God-forsaken country. ' Just get me the hell out of here. I'm bored to death,' said the princess. She quickly packed 35 suitcases (20 for shoes alone) and headed to the ramshackle, rat- infested bus station to catch the next overcrowded, mechanically unsound tour bus to the Alps.

"On the sixteen hour bus trip (non-stop), the princess could hardly contain her excitement. For most of the trip, she was trying to talk to the passengers who kept telling her to shut her big fat mouth for they were trying to get some sleep and no one could understand what the hell she was saying anyway. You see, though her mother and father understood and could speak a small bit of English as well as other some European languages, they never considered that their daughter would benefit from learning another language besides Borinese since the kingdom no longer received dignitaries (nor common street derelicts, expensive vacuum cleaner salesmen, Seventh Day Adventists, and the such) from other countries. This saved the kingdom quite a bit of money since they did not have to have any foreign reading materials nor radio or television transmissions brought in to the country. The were all quite content reading the one page (printed on one side), monthly newsletter produced by one of the king's chefs who so longed to be a writer. This was all the news that they needed to have.

"As she gazed out the of the bus window, hours later, she saw the mountains and screamed, in Borinese, at the top of her lungs, 'Holy bucket of weasel shit!! Look at those rocks!! This is going to be absolutely fantastic!!' At this point, one of the male passengers folded up the newspaper (from some other country—quite a few pages, actually) he was reading, quietly got out of his seat and slugged the princess right in the middle of her ugly face, rendering her unconscious for the remainder of the trip.

"Hurray!!" shouted the passengers in unison.

"She was starting to come to just as the bus pulled into the resort. After the bus driver gave her a few quick hits of some very powerful smelling salts (of the same type that doctors across the world have been known to use to revive individuals whose hearts have stopped when a high voltage defibrillator was not immediately available)—and a couple of slaps across the face and a knee to the stomach just because—she was almost totally lucid. She did manage to get all her suitcases off the bus and into the Switzerland Econlodge and Highly Unstable Nitroglycerin and Explosives Detonation Center. After checking in, which was very difficult as no one spoke Borinese, she went into the lodge area where she noticed everyone lounging around, drinking and laughing, carrying skis and poles. She looked out the window and saw people coming down the mountain on the skis and was quite excited to do this herself.

" 'Oh, yeah!! This is something I gotta try!!' she screamed (in Borinese) so loud and in such a high pitch that a number of the tourists clutched their ears and collapsed from the loss of equilibrium and a few hundred helium balloons from a children's birthday party exploded simultaneously. Amidst a number of skiers moaning from the pain pulsating in their heads and the deafening howls of frightened and hysterical children, she ran off to the ski supply store to get the necessary equipment used in the sport.

"When the salesman asked her what she wanted, she pointed out the window at the skiers and then down at her, shall we say, less than ideal body. The salesman correctly assumed that the lady wanted to buy the entire works. She quickly tried on vast quantities of boots, skis, jackets, gloves and the like manufactured of every conceivable material (and with every bit of modern technology) known to man, in every style ever made. After roughly three hours, she had a complete outfit, including a lift ticket good for 12 years, a tall Cat in the Hat ski cap made from a combination eel skin/cow udder material, and super ski boots (made of a newly developed polymer that had been known to cause diaper rash in laboratory chickens) that could be made into a spacious, air tight, water repellent, sleeping bag with a few quick zipper adjustments. With most of her money gone (the minister of finance had contacted the largest of the Swiss banks and had been able to convert the Borinese currency—which resembled multi-colored, plastic poker chips—into Swiss francs at a conversion rate of 75,000 Borinese Claklas to 1 franc), she was ready to hit the slopes.

"Before the princess left the shop, the exasperated—though quite content from making such a big commission—salesman was trying to ask the princess if she knew how to ski. The princess, not understanding any other language than Borinese, and 'hello', 'goodbye', and 'wanna fuck' in English was baffled. The salesman asked her in about 15 different languages, including Swahili and an extremely obscure Mongolian dialect used by about 35 people in the outer most reaches of Tibet, but still couldn't get through. He then pointed outside and told her to get out.

" 'Get the hell out of my store, you crazy bitch!' said the salesman. The princess did just that, smiling all the way.

"The princess walked over to the ski lift area and was very confused to say the least. She didn't know why people got on these contraptions and where they were headed. And she certainly didn't know how to get on one. She saw all the different slopes around her and couldn't decide which one to go on. 'Crap in a bucket of piss! This is a pain in my royal ass,' said the princess.

"She approached a nearby member of the ski patrol who was leaning against a tree, holding his head in both his gloved hands and tried to ask what him to do. The ski patrol member, who was suffering from a horrendous Tequila and Mad Dog hangover, was on the verge of pummeling her with punches if she didn't stop her incessant whining in a foreign language. He just pointed to the third lift from the right. The 'This Will Surely Kill You or at Least Shatter a Few Bones and Damage Some Necessary Internal Organs Beyond Any Possible Repair' slope lift. Although nearly falling to her death several times, she did manage to hang onto the lift chair long enough to make it to the top of the slope (the super, electro magnets imbedded in her newly purchased ski gloves kept her hands firmly planted to the lift chair while the powerful magnetic field generated caused the watches of several skiers on nearby lifts to explode) and headed to the beginning of the course. Her new gloves were still attached to the lift chair and were causing interruptions in radio transmissions and showing up as unidentified blips on nearby air traffic controllers' radar screens as she shuffled along to the start area along with a few other, professional and Olympic level skiers.

"She hadn't quite figured out how to get started, so she stood and observed the others for a while. She came to the conclusion that all one must do is lean forward and simply let gravity do the rest. So she went to the starting area, leaned over as far as she possibly could and shot down the hill, gaining speed with every inch. She thought that this was all very exciting as the adrenaline coursed through her veins and the wind began drying and chafing her fragile, princess skin, but she did wonder what would happen if she had to steer or perhaps even stop. 'Maybe I won't have to steer or stop,' said the stupid princess out loud to herself.

"The members of the ski patrol were laying around, getting a late winter tan and trying to recover from the all night pill popping and drinking binge they had the previous evening to the point where they at least could stand up straight without swaying back and forth too much, when one of them noticed the Princess racing down the hill at an incredible rate of speed. They were all wondering if she was a show off or an acrobat, the way she was lifting one leg then the other.

"I've never seen anything like that before in my life." said one of the older patrol members.

"I think I saw a clown smacked on angel dust, aerosol fumes and industrial fungicides do that on the bunny slope at the 'Ski with the Freaks and Carnies Festival' last year," said another, " I think they had to shoot him with three shots of a mega-dose rhino tranquilizer just to get him into the straight jacket."

"All of them thought she was doing great, the way she seemed to maintain her balance while bending over and flailing both her arms and legs. What they didn't know was that the skis she had purchased came equipped with small electric motors, a complex micro-hydraulic piston system and precision, military grade gyroscopes that virtually guaranteed that the skis will always remain on an even keel no matter the circumstances. It really did appear that the Princess knew what she was doing—and doing it quite well, at that!

"Only one of them noticed that she was headed directly for a very large tree and at the rate of speed she was traveling, there would be no way she could avoid hitting it. Especially if she continued to do those crazy stunts. With this in mind, the brave and still partially drunk and 'hopped up' ski patrol member headed down the hill in an attempt to save the bored, ugly, dyed clown red hair princess from a certain doom.

"Ulab, the ski patrol member who was trying to save the princess' life, was a member of the newly organized 'Giving Hope—Though Not a Whole Heck of a Lot—to Those About to be Dashed to Pieces' slope patrol. All he kept saying to himself as he raced down the slope was, 'Keep the bitch from hitting the tree. Keep the bitch from hitting the tree.' As he closed the distance between him and the princess, he actually thought he would save her from splattering into the tree. The gap narrowed even more and he would reach her within a few seconds.

"Keep the bitch from hitting the tree. Keep the bitch from hitting the tree," he kept muttering.

"The princess, on the other hand, was having so much fun, she didn't even see the massive tree looming in front of her. Ulab yelled to her and she turned around. 'Look out for the fucking tree!! Turn! Turn!' Being the princess couldn't understand anything except the word 'fucking', thought that this guy was trying to pick her up. She smiled with that crooked mouth full of yellowing, spaciously gapped, irregularly shaped teeth and waved to him. Ulab just pointed ahead and the princess turned forward again and managed to finally see the tremendous tree.

" 'Dammit it all to hell!! Shit! I was having such a good time, too!!' yelled the princess in that horrendously screechy voice as she expected to be crushed against the tree at any moment. That magnificently piercing voice of hers also managed to cause an avalanche that wiped out the ski lodge and a greater portion of the small town that was in the midst of its 'Ain't It Great To Be Alive' festival.

"The gap was closed to a matter of feet and there was very little time to spare. Seconds before she was about to hit the tree, Ulab lifted his pole and shoved the princess away from the looming tree. Ulab felt wonderful–whether it was from performing a feat of heroism or a minor flashback from the previous evening's drug and booze indulgence wasn't immediately apparent to Ulab. Then he realized that while he may have saved the princess from hitting the tree, he sent her on a direct path to go over the cliff, which she did, plummeting to her death."

"Oh, that's just wonderful! " said Ulab, "that's the fifth one this season. Crap! That's it! Right after the big 'Guzzlefest and Capsule Munching' bash on Saturday, I'm gonna gradually reduce—over an indeterminate amount of time—my drinking, taking pills and smoking Turkish Hashish!"

"And the moral of our story: It is certainly Much, Much Better to be Bored to Death Than Actually Dying."

The credits start rolling and I look out the window of the classroom and see this clown running by the window being chased by a bull. Anabella!! This is goofy, I'm thinking to myself. The teacher still hasn't come back from the toilet or wherever, and the girl in the room with me is still snoozing or in a coma so I decided to leave. I turned the TV off and headed out the door. I look down the hall and see Tom coming towards me walking on stilts.

"Hey, look at me!! I had a tremendous growth spurt!!" shouted Tom from down the hall.

As he got closer, I told him that he did not have a growth spurt at all and that he was walking on stilts. He denied that he was on stilts, claiming that he had this miraculous, intense period of growth in a matter of an hour or so.

"Look," I said, "unless this growth spurt involved the actual flesh and bones of your legs turning into pieces of knotty, warped and splintered 2 by 4's, you're on stilts. Look. You got a freakin nail sticking out of your calf!"

"No way!" replied Tom, "I had a major growth spurt! I'm going to show Bolten."

This I had to see, so I followed him as he walked in that long, awkward gait that people who wear stilts walk in, down to the guidance counselor's office. When we got there, the office was empty and busted up. The computer was smashed and smoldering, papers thrown about, chairs splintered on the floor. Looked like someone had just come in and gone crazy. I looked at Tom, thinking for a minute that it was he. Then I saw a sheet of printout on the desk. I picked it up and immediately recognized it as a career path choice report from the super computer. And the name at the top was that of Mr. Bolten! He had done one on himself.

I scanned down the paper while Tom tried to stand still, crouching down to keep his head from hitting the ceiling without toppling over. According to the super computer, Bolten's career path should be…

"A con artist. Self-Employed. Primary responsibility is to bamboozle people by telling them what they want to hear in order for personal gain. Requires the spouting of words that don't mean anything, but believed by those you tell them to. Will spend time in and out of correctional/mental institutions."

"I knew that Bolten was full of crap!" shouted Tom before falling off the stilts and landing on the desk.

Yeah, I thought, me too. As we headed out into the hallway, Anabella still dressed like a rodeo clown came running by us being chased by that bull. I tried to yell to her to tell her that she doesn't have to be a rodeo clown anymore, but she disappeared around the corner. Oh well, I thought, maybe she'll be a damn good clown. Just then the fire alarm went off and I woke up.

I looked over to my Kmart LED clock and it showed it was 2:38 am. Two minutes?! The whole dream took two minutes. Well, that dream restored my faith in my research and I vowed that I would continue—no matter what intense intestinal pain, general discomfort, and the incredible taxing of my overall bodily functions that I would certainly incur from my eating habits—with my highly scientific dream studies. After all, this dream came to being by eating a chicken salad, oyster, bacon fat, pork rind, mayonnaise, soy sauce, lettuce, parsley, garlic, onion, beets, spaghetti, carrot, lentil bean, pepper, Worcester sauce, rice, peanut butter and pepperoni hero sandwich dipped in baked bean sauce..

    *   *   *   *   *   *   *

Now, I simply love seafood, if it's fresh and cooked well enough to destroy all that harmful bacteria. You know, the kind that eats off various limbs or makes your head expand so much that you need to carry around a shoehorn so you can get your softball cap on. And the only real way to get fresh fish is to catch it yourself. As kids, we used to go fishing almost everyday in the summer. We would get worms the night before by digging up the neighbor's award winning, foul smelling, gassy compost heap. Whatever the hell he was composting, we didn't care, the worms we got were as big as chicken legs! We would make sure our tackle boxes had enough hooks—complete with bits and pieces of all our flesh—and line and all that other crap you need to go fishing. Including the rusted pair of pliers needed to wrench the hooks out of the god-forsaken fish we caught or out of each other's bodies.

The next day we'd all head down through the mosquito and tic infested woods to the slimy, polluted river that contained various heavy metals, chunks of partially processed soap emulsifiers, grade F industrial sludge and 250,000% of the daily recommended allowance of Mercury and Arsenic. In 1975 it was the named "The Densest River in Pennsylvania." There was a very small parade —with a circus monkey with mange and two drunk clowns who were stopping every so many yards to either puke or pee— and a picnic to honor the occasion. Later in life I had found, after inquiring about the "Old Fishing Spot" to one of my longtime friends, that the river was so dense that it had actually solidified and was now being used as a combination drag strip/street hockey site.

We would spend the whole muggy and sweltering day trying to catch slimy, bottom feeding, muck sucking fish. We would usually end up fighting about something and go home with fish hooks in our arms and legs—and with only a couple of fish, which my mother would freeze for use at a later date. My mother was the "Queen" of freezing stuff. She still has those poor, little, pitiful fish in her freezer along with frozen bits of luncheon meats, bread crusts and soups brought over to "this country" in 1958. "Ima no gonna waste any of God's food (pronounced like "hood")!!" We always said that maybe she should give it back to God since we weren't going to eat it, which prompted her to chase us around the house with "the wooden spoon" or the red belt with metal rivets on it, threatening to call St. Gabriel's Hall—the local reform school—and have them send a bus to pick us up since she wasn't going to drive us to the place where they kept "the rotten kids of the Devil." She still makes the sign of the cross and sprinkles Holy water on her head whenever she drives by the place.

My father took us deep-sea fishing during one of those summers. Being kids, we relished the thought of spending the day on a boat floating miles from the coast in the blazing sun with 300 people—all drunk and suffering from 2nd and 3rd degree burns—getting their lines tangled and threatening to kill the captain. My father was pretty excited as well. He went out and spent $175 on a new deep-sea fishing pole with "Magna–Pull" reel. It looked really neat! Just like the kind they use on those fake-fishing shows where the professional angler reels in a humongous fish that isn't moving. He also made about 45 sandwiches–"You never know, we might get shipwrecked! And I'll be damned if I going to start eating people! The meat is too damn tough! Do you want mustard on your sandwich?"—for our excursion.

The next day, at 6 am, we arrived at the boat and got our gear from the captain. Everybody, of course, except Dad. He had all this new stuff, and held his head up in cocky pride as he paraded in front of all the rest of us schmucks with the cheap, bent, bowed and splintered rental gear. Well, the trip out to the fishing spot—the famous wreck of the HMS Whyamistillafloat—took about 20 minutes during which time we all enjoyed 7 or 8 of the sandwiches. The captain dropped anchor and said that it was okay to cast the lines. Everybody scrambled like a bunch of piglets struggling to get to one of their mother's many teats trying to find a spot for all their own. My father staked out a spot at the rear of the boat when we first got on and we all had to inhale diesel fumes the whole way to the site. My Dad had turned blue and vomited over the side of the boat before the captain threw the anchor out, but now he was just a little green and was ready to fish.

My father goes to cast his line; the bottom of the pole hits the rear railing of the boat, falls out of his hand and into the Atlantic Ocean. Everybody kind of stood around and watched with smirks on their faces as the fantastic and magnificent fishing contraption that had never even been used slowly sank. My Dad was devastated. He just watched for a few minutes. We had just started fishing and he would now have to rent gear if he wanted to do something to occupy his time for the next 6 hours. He rented the second rate, nearly defective stuff and we fished for 6 hrs. We caught two miniature sea bass, some sort of rock looking fish and a license plate from North Dakota. And it only put my Dad out $300 plus.

One summer, many years later, my father had this big fish cookout. He invited all the relatives and their children and their friends and pets from the tri-county area, and had a whole boatload of fish and seafood products ready to be barbecued. He had clams, shrimp, lobster, and bluefish—the fish that is so fishy tasting even cats say "What? You expect me to eat that piece of crap? Give me a friggin bowl of milk or I'll scratch your eyes out!" The place looked like a riot scene—billowing white smoke from the ethyl alcohol injected charcoal grill and kids running around like savage animals. Loads of fun!

My father cooked all this stuff (to what degree of safety is still in question—I thought for a brief moment that I saw my cousin's lips swell up like balloons, but he was just kidding around) and we ate the fish, sampling everything that was put on the grill that had once lived in the sea and drank warm beer. The thought of it still makes me sick to my stomach. I believe at some point during the picnic I began hallucinating. I went around collecting the wet, malodorous, discarded clamshells mumbling something about being the richest person in Bedrock. I then felt this overwhelming wave of nausea and ran to grab a draw of the industrial strength stomach medicine from the keg in the kitchen. Not feeling too well, I decided that I needed to go to sleep. I stumbled into bed and immediately fell asleep. And immediately started dreaming.

In this particular dream, I am out with several of my friends. We are sitting in this semi-fancy (they have linen tablecloths, but plastic forks) restaurant and everyone is just talking about nothing in particular, but from the cacophonous and fragmented conversations I gather that we are going to eat then go to a movie. I picked up a menu and start to look it over while my friends continue to drink these black and red concoctions from fish bowl size brandy glasses. I'm kind of hoping to hear what movie we are going to see, but no one seemed to make mention of it. Somebody started talking about her new job at the newly opened "Dance, Dammit, Dance!" Interpretive clog dancing instructional facility. She mentioned that we could stop by and see the place before we head out to the movies. Then everyone started chattering again and I couldn't really make anything out. So I opened the terribly oversized menu (2 ft x 3 ft) and took a gander at what this apparently popular (all the tables were full) eatery had to offer.

On the inside of the gigantic menu was a greeting from the owners.

"Welcome to the one and only, exclusive Egret Club. There is no other dining establishment or experience like this in the world. We hope that our world-renowned eatery makes a lasting impression of the type of mentality you're dealing with. Please enjoy our varied selections of exotic foods, enjoy our very unique list of liquid libations, enjoy our superb surroundings, and most of all, please, enjoy yourselves. We pride ourselves in providing the best service to you, our most beloved patrons. Because that is what living is all about. And if you encounter any problems at all with the food or service, don't bother us, okay, as we are way too busy. Please, you aren't stupid people; figure it out yourself. Thank you, The Management."

Well, I had never seen a greeting like this before and thought it to be highly unusual, yet funny. I said out loud to no one in particular, "Hey you gotta see this!" But everyone was too busy laughing and drinking and talking about how this guy (where one of my friends works) got his fingers glued to the sole of his Italian loafers and they had to call the fire department to free him. From what I was able to gather, the gentleman lost most of his finger to the bone, but the Italian loafers were just fine. Oh well, I thought, and went back to reading the menu.

Appetizers:
(One should always eat a little something before you actually sit down and eat)

   1). Sloppers...$2.00
      Sautéed Jamaican weasel brains with oregano and cheese
      puffs spread on stale pieces of moldy bread.
      With cheese..$1.00 extra.

   2). Vision Tidbits..$1.95
      Irregular particles of baby Snow Harp seal eyeballs, tossed with
      Eastern Dairy Cow nostrils, sheep ligaments and sand. Served
      with a big Wastebasket of nacho chips and our famous
      "Somebody! Please! Shoot Me Between the Eyes 'Cause I'm
      Dying Here!!" Hot sauce.

   3). Black Surprise...$3.00
      Minced Mongolian tarantula with diced onionskin and tomato
      seeds mixed with liquefied carpet fibers served in kiln roasted
      Scorpion shells.

   4). Walk a Mile...$3.95
      Boneless Arabian camel hooves, lightly battered with our special
      mix made from colored Halloween corn, poppy seeds and gristle.
      Served with fondue style processed cheese facsimile in an
      Ethiopian Black Rhino skull.

   5). Man's Best Friend...$1.75
      Lightly roasted AKC certified Dalmatian tails and sweet and sour
      Australian Dingo tongue sautéed in Botswanian Bush Mud.
      Served with a dog bone shaped imitation biscuit manufactured
      from warped Particleboard and glue.

I was beginning to feel a bit sick to my stomach, but was compelled to keep reading.

Soups:
(All our soups are carefully and meticulously prepared here in our wonderfully spacious, immaculate, and efficient kitchens...unless they are made somewhere else.)

1). Necking Soup.................................$.89/cup...$.90/gallon
    Sumptuous African Giraffe neck and seawater seasoned with just a dash of salt, a pinch of pepper and hint of household disinfectant.

2). Breathe Easy..$2.50/bowl
    Creamed Mexican Chihuahua lung and minced Himalayan goat sweat glands in a Hyena based bouillon lightly seasoned with our own brand of seasoning, including, but not limited to: road salt, pepper, thyme, MSG, habanera pepper, insulin, mouthwash, and chocolate sprinkles.

3). Blackboard Soup...$8.50/bowl
    Freshly quarried New England Chalk boiled in Siamese cat blood. Served in a child's plastic beach bucket with stale cubes of imitation bread, otherwise known as croutons.

Salads:
(We only use the finest ingredients in OUR salads. We use anything we want in the salads we serve YOU)

1). Poison Sumac and Oak Salad.....................................$2.37
    Served with the House Calamine dressing. Bring a little of the pain and inflammatory itch of the great outdoors into your digestive tract.

2). Tossed Ground Eggshells and Wood Mulch w/ Endive......$1.69
Served in a big Hobo Boot with forks that resemble garden rakes. Sprinkled with pulverized Bo weevils and shredded mosquitoes.

3). Shredded Plastic and Strips of Shoe Leather...................$3.00
Grade D, malformed and mis—manufactured particles of plastic tossed with remains of discarded, foul smelling bowling shoes. Served in the hubcap of a 1963 Chevy Impala.

4). Tossed Chinese Paper Balloons and Used Pen Caps.........$2.75
Delicately hand crafted, decorative, and fragile works of colored paper (dyed in dioxins) combined with coarse, irregular, and indigestible used pen caps. And some sprouts.

All salads come with the following dressing choices:
    *Blood *Tar *Whipped Shoe Polish *Liquefied Sweet Tarts*
    *Liquid Nitrogen *Airline Fuel *Rendered Baboon Fat *

My stomach was really grumbling and I wanted my friends to look at this menu! I looked up from the large piece of folded laminated cardboard and my friends were still laughing about the guy who had his fingers stuck to his shoe. They looked extremely drunk and were smoking cigarettes one right after the other. Johnny had an extra large, black Italian Olive—the kind with the pit in—stuck in his nose and was trying to blow it out by clogging up one nostril with his thumb and trying to expel air through the other. He was turning beet red and had tears rolling down one cheek. My friend keeps telling all of us that we really do need to see the dance place she works at. She mentioned something about it being the only place like it on earth. No one was particularly listening to her. I couldn't imagine what was so interesting about this place. I went back to the menu.

Pasta:
(All of our pasta entrees come with a choice of a vegetable—sugar beets from dented and rusted cans)

1). Meat Ravioli...$12.79
Delicious ground Amazonian Gorilla fingers stuffed into a hearty, moldy, tough, synthetic dough exterior. Smothered in a thick jellyfish—like substance that has been dyed red with tattoo ink to make it look somewhat appetizing—if you have eye problems or have been Hypnotized into believing so.

2). Spaghetti (made from highly bleached grains and stuff) and your choice of:
* Shattered Clam Shells.............................$7.57
* Sharpened Chicken Beaks........................$6.43
* Succulent Octopus Suction Cups............$15.26
* Ground Diseased Ostrich Liver...............$3.50
* Pureed Wasp Stingers.............................$1.24
* Duckbill Platypus Skin Sausage.............$27.43

3). Lasagna...$15.95
Ground Mutant African Mud snake and powdered White elephant tusks smothered in a synthetic tomato-like (it's red) sauce. Topped with grated Mongolian Zebra Cheese.

Seafood:
(All of our seafood comes from the water—well, most of it anyways.)

1). Boiled Crab Spleens...............................$4.92
Rotten, festering crab spleens smothered in a sweet yellow, pus-like sauce served in blackened and shattered crab shells. Also

served with a side of partially clean coleslaw and a loaf of solid-ified radon gas.

2). Big Fish Surprise...$10.64
Shredded Beluga Whale intestine, creamed King shrimp brains, and diced Baltic Sea octopus tentacles carefully blended with Warehouse surplus sea monkeys served in a Hammerhead Shark skull. Comes with a choice of a baked orange, a micro waved avocado, or a vomit bag.

3). Big Bite..$3.47
Filet of Great White shark skin seasoned with sea salt, potassium benzoate, and dandelion seeds served on a stale, crusty croissant smeared with rancid, curdled mayonnaise.

4). Big Ray...$56.24
A boiled 537lb (weight before boiling—actually weighs more when served due to the additional water) Killer Manta Ray stuffed with suckerfish, piranha teeth, Sea sponges and some sort of seaweed/plankton/anthrax formulated substance from an epicurean experiment gone horribly wrong we found in the kitchen. Comes with a side of smashed jackass lips. Served on a big plate.

Meat:
(All of our meats come from animals…except the synthetic stuff we sometimes manufacture in our laboratories…ah……..kitchens)

1). Deep Fried Burro Leg..$16.95
Two, old and tough burro legs, heavily breaded and deep-fried in lard and Vaseline. Comes with French fried hamster earlobes, pinto parts and Coleslaw.

2). Roast Gallbladder..$14.95
   Delicious roasted Bull elephant gallbladder with creamed
   Australian Emus sauce, burnt potatoes and something resembling a salad—if Salads didn't have lettuce, or tomatoes or anything else you would typically find in a salad.

3). Steaks:
   -All steaks are cooked over a grate that serves as a protective grill
   placed over the steam release tower of the Limerick nuclear
   power plant so various Species of birds don't fly in and become
   extinct and served with hallucinogenic mushrooms and angel
   dust sauce; no substitutions-
   * Whale Shark Steak.......................................$14.93
   * Old Buffalo (@1893)....................................$13.26
   * Vulture Steak..$49.75
   * Jackal Flank Steak.......................................$25.19
   * Gorilla Chest Steak......................................$114.13

4). Aroma Delight..$2.35
   Minced Wood skunk stuffed into Sewer rat intestine served with
   French fried Pygmy raccoon eyes and deep-fried Idaho hog jowls.
   * This meal will be served only in one our hermetically sealed
   Eating chambers*

Desserts:
(All of our special desserts are made)

1). Yak a la Santee...$2.65
   Pulverized, young Andes yak muscles covered with whipped
   cold cream and assorted old fruit and large curd cottage cheese.
   Served in a broken light bulb.

2). Armadillo Dough Cakes...$1.53
   Ground Texas Armadillo carcasses mixed with lead, road tar, dough and jagged shards of sugar cane. Served on a slab of tire retread.

3).Moose head...$16.75
   Old Canadian Moose head smothered in real, synthetic chocolate and volatile, and highly unstable liquid corrosives. Doused in Kentucky bourbon and topped with small leaf Bok choi, organically grown in pig waste.

Beverages:

1). Frozen, Bitter coffee...$.75
2). Solidified Bloods (For the little bit of Vampire in all of us!!):
   *Baby Zebra...$1.00
   *Research Monkey...$1.95
   *Anemic Emus...$3.12
   *Japanese Blowfish...$1.12
   *Common Street Dog..$4.23

3) Teas (Brewed in a rusty kettle with hyper-chlorinated, heavy water with exceptionally large microorganisms floating around.)
   *Mongolian Liver Tea...$1.25
   *Ginseng, Ginkgo Boloba, Yohimbe Bark, Guarana, Echinacea and Marshmallow Root—served in a 10-gallon wastebasket..$1.26
   *Diluted Battery acid...$2.47
   *Hashish and Chloroform—served in a souvenir thimble...$4.31

4). Carbonated Beverages (We use only tainted nitrogen in our crude and highly unsafe Carbonation process)

*Moo Pop...$1.09
Our special blend of Grade X milk, large curd cottage cheese and Yogurt in a super carbonated suspension.

*V318 Cocktail Soda.......................................$2.84
A superb carbonated concoction made from 318 different vegetables, weeds, grasses, mulches and tree buds.

*Smooth Flow...$2.60
Carbonated industrial degreaser with a hint of lime and a dash of mustard.

*Jose Manachoco's Amazing and Fantastic Seltzer Tonic...$.75
A marvelous blend of carbonated, de—ionized and bleached, gutter water, sulfur, copper and little bits of shattered corn chips kept crispy because they are coated in wax from manufacturer -rejected children's birthday candles.

At this point, even though what I had read wasn't exceptionally appetizing, I was feeling hungry and put down the menu to see if anyone was ready to order any food. I looked at the table and it was piled high with empty and dirty dishes, animal bones, skins and teeth, multicolored sauces and a cup of rendered baboon fat that was being used as an ashtray with about 30 cigarette butts smoldering, giving off a horrible smell. It dawned on me that my friends had not only ordered, but had eaten while I was reading the menu. I asked out loud to anyone why they hadn't asked me if I wanted anything to eat. Slaggy said that they had asked several times, but that I had ignored them, being totally engrossed in the menu. Well, that was just dandy.

The waiter came to the table (he looked an awful like Sebastian Cabot—and sounded just like him) and asked in a snooty and sarcastic voice, "Have you finished stuffing yourselves, distending your stomachs like large helium balloons, or would you prefer I go bother the cooks and their group of technicians to manufacture some more food for you?" Everyone at the table was groaning the groans of people who have eaten way too much. They were not going to be eating anymore. "Very well then, you group of bloated farm animals, I have the check here for you. Which one of you will have the pleasure of paying me?" For some reason, everyone pointed to me and the waiter handed me the check.

And for some reason, I took it! The waiter stood there waiting with his hand out and his eyes up at the ceiling as if the thought of looking at me was making him ill. I looked at the bill, which was about a foot and a half long, and saw the total for all the food and beverages—$107.15. Well, the bill didn't seem that bad for all they had consumed, and me, not even thinking twice about that I had not eaten one bite and was starving, pulled out my wallet, ready to pay the man. I searched through my cash supply and found that all I had were one thousand dollar bills. I had never seen a thousand dollar bill before, which probably explains why that instead of a president on the face of the bill, it had the smiling face of Ella Fitzgerald, with the motto "That's right, baby. It's in God We Trust. Oh, you gotta know that's true!" encircling that gleaming, smiling face.

I mentioned to the waiter that all I had were thousands. He looked as if I had told him that the toilet in the men's room had overflowed and the wet, shit—stained toilet paper had reached his shoes. "Well, you certainly don't expect me to try and make change for that, do you? How someone could possibly be so ignorant to even expect me to do such petty work is beyond human comprehension. It boggles the mind, it truly does."

I told the waiter that if he wants to get paid, I am going to have to go out to get change. He snorted through his nose, rolled his eyes skyward, muttered, "Simply unbelievable!" and quickly turned around and walked away. I turned to tell my friends that I am going out to get change but they are all sleeping in their chairs, heads back, mouths agape, and all the guys with their belt buckles loosened, pants unbuttoned and fly's unzipped. I looked around the restaurant and EVERYBODY there was in the same condition. I began to think that perhaps it was a good thing that I didn't eat anything.

I got up and headed to the front of the restaurant. As I walked by the entrance, I saw a big bowl of mints and, being that I was hungry, grabbed a handful, just glancing at the big red label on the bowl -

Jeremiah Wallabashov's Miraculous and Rejuvenating Breath Solids
Manufactured in Zimbabwe from the finest, used, Industrial Air
Fresheners—the same type used to make a cattle slaughter
house in Arizona on a hot August afternoon smell as pleasant as
a backed -up septic system in Arizona on a cool October
morning—partially hydrogenated cottonseed oil, and Pinesap.

I walked out the door and headed to the old brick building next door. It had a colorfully lit glass front door with the image of Fred Astaire etched in it. I opened the door and walked into a large room that looked like a massive school gymnasium floor. There were people wearing wooden clogs milling around and they all started looking me, scrunching their noses. They had evidently discovered my pocket of wonderful breath solids. Then some tall, skinny guy wearing black tights, red satin shirt and blue wooden clogs, who I assumed was the leader or director, yelled into a police megaphone (in a gravelly, highly effeminate voice, like Harvey Firestein),

"Listen people! Look at me! Over here!! Please ignore the smelly gentleman who decided to grace us with his foul presence. We can all thank him later for making our eyes water and making us feel sick to our collective stomachs…It's time to dance, dammit, dance! Snap snap!! Places people, places!! For the love of God, why don't you people listen to me?

Please don't ignore me when I yell at you!! It makes me want to cry....almost! Somebody please grab my migraine pills!? I feel a spell coming on! Sansachacca, do I look bloated to you? Good Lord, I feel like a cow that drank Lake Michigan!"

I gathered that this was the "Dance, Dammit, Dance" place where my friend worked. Everyone slowly turned away from looking at me and went to the opposite wall from me. Some were doing knee bends and some were on the floor stretching their muscles. Others were rolling their necks and some had their eyes closed, mumbling unintelligible words in what appeared to be a form of meditation. After a few moments of this, they all stood up, shoulder to shoulder in a single line of humans facing me. The director walked to the center of the line, and facing the group—a mere two or three feet from him—began yelling into the megaphone.

"Okay people now! Let's have the line nice and straight!! Do you think we could that? For me? Please? Sometime in the next two or three minutes would be real peachy. Come on now! We have a lot to do!! And I went and talked to maintenance, and they are going to turn up the fans as soon as they get back from their union mandated post—dinner, pre—desert cigarette break, okay, and that stench won't make our eyes burn anymore I promise! Okay, are we almost ready?! Okay, Lakachankalina, hit it with the music, girl!! Oh, God, I have cramps!"

Tremendously loud techno-music began thundering from four massive speakers suspended from the ceiling by cables. The group then began some sort of dance where they would tap the clog and slide forward a step, tap the clog, and slide back a step. Not much of dance, I thought to myself. Then the music got louder and the tempo quickened. They were now just tapping the clog of the left foot, not bothering with the slide step. As the music intensified, so did the tapping. It was now more stomping the clog shod left foot than tapping. And the music was getting louder! I could see splinters flying up from the floor as it was being pounded by scores of clog wielding fanatics. And they pounded harder!! Ten or so of the "dancers" had shattered their wooden clogs and were on the floor grabbing their ankles, the music too loud to hear their howls of agony.

I was getting a little frightened of this place and was thinking, what the hell kind of job could my friend possibly have here? About six more people fell, their shinbones poking through their skin. Two more were sitting with their left leg bending the opposite way as their knees had simply "blown out". More were splintering and shattering their clogs and collapsing, grabbing various parts of the foot and leg, faces strained in immense pain. I remember thinking that I wasn't probably going to get change for a thousand dollar bill in here.

I decided to leave just as the music stopped and the director came running in yelling through the megaphone, " What the hell do you think your doing?! We are supposed to be dancing!! Dance, Dammit, Dance!! Remember?! Not, let's break up the dance floor, dammit, let's break up the dance floor!! Oh my God, what happened to you?! Is that your foot?! Oh, Jesus, that looks horrible! Have you all lost your minds!!? Tap, tap, and slide…tap, tap, and slide!! Not stomp…stomp…break a clog and shatter a bone…stomp!! Oh, my head is splitting!! I must call my therapist!! Rennailotsa, girl, get me my phone…better yet, be a fuzzy peach and make the call, okay?"

I walked out of the building and saw a tremendous amount of commotion outside the restaurant. There were police vehicles, ambulances, and fire trucks blocking the street. People were running around in a panic and trying to cross the police barriers set up around the restaurant. People yelling, bullhorns bellowing and that awfully annoying static, police radio noise filled the air. I stood and watched as the front doors of the restaurant open and animals commence coming out as if in some sort of circus parade or some big, well produced, recreation of the loading of animals on Noah's Ark.

A huge elephant comes out first, followed by the rest of the animals—both domestic and exotic—down the walkway to the street, making loud noises and defecating on the pavement. Then out of nowhere, Captain Kangaroo, in his sharp outfit, comes running towards the police line, yelling at the top of his lungs....

"Please!! Please!! Can someone help me!! Please!! Has anyone seen my cigarettes? I can't find the goddamn things!! Jesus Christ, I need a smoke!!...Oh my God!! Look at that!! Will you look at that?! Look at that zebra? Can you believe someone would eat that animal? Unbelievable!! Everyone knows zebra meat is way too tough after they turn 2 or 3!! They would have to marinate that beast for about three weeks in a mellow balsamic vinegar and virgin, first—pressed, olive oil based—with crushed garlic and rosemary—marinade!! Maybe a twist of lime!! And that would only make it bearable to eat!! For the love of God!! What's the matter with these people?! Anyone have a fucking cigarette?! Shit!! Come on!! I'll pay you a quarter for a smoke!! Anyone?! Ah, fuck it!!"

I managed to peak into the window of the restaurant and noticed that there were no people in there. I imagined that all the patrons had been roused from their slumber by the ruckus outside and left as quickly as possible. I couldn't see my friends anywhere amongst the crowd and figured that they had headed to the movie theater and that I would meet them there.

I started walking down the street, not knowing where I was going. I make the turn around the corner of the building and start falling! I fell through a manhole cover!!...I shoot straight up out of bed with my heart thumping like a drum!! I run downstairs to the kitchen for a cool glass of water and another long draw of the super stomach medication from the kitchen keg.

* * * * * * * * * * * * * *

In this particular dream, I was at the fair with some friends of mine. This was the Fireman's Fair, the same one that has been coming to town every summer—just as school let out—for about 35 years. Each year, for two weeks, this fantastic and magical spectacle of rusted, defective and squeaky circus rides (all in a state of horrible disrepair), carnival freaks, bacteria laden cotton candy and midway games—where if you're lucky you can bring home a goldfish in a plastic sandwich bag, only to have it die 47 minutes after you get it home—came and graced our town with its magnificent presence. It was the place to be. All the friends you would only see in school are there, greeting each other like it's been months since they have seen each other when in fact it had been less than 72 hours.

There is really nothing like strolling on dirt paths worn into the grass midway, smelling the stench of animals and munching on a "carnies' " corn dog manufactured from bits and pieces of highly stressed animals that were no longer able to cut the mustard on the grueling carnival trail and corn meal made with what farmers call "I Really Think We Should Think Twice About Shipping This Stuff Out—We Could Go To Jail" corn, shoved onto a pointy, used Popsicle stick and served to you by an individual that looks as if he all he can eat is pureed water.

In the dream, our group was walking around the trailer that served waffle and ice cream sandwiches, boiled walnuts, fried sugar patties, and salt licks. We saw one of the tough guys from school trying to impress his date by attempting to ring the bell at the sledgehammer—slam attraction. He was spitting in his hands then rubbing them together as she looked on adoringly. He put on a real serious look on and says, "Honey, you better stand back. I need room, baby!"

Well, evidently she didn't listen. He swung the sledgehammer back and smacked her right in the mouth. She crumpled to the ground as he continued with his attempt to ring the bell. He hit the mark and the metal slide went up approximately 7 inches. "Shit! Let me try again!" he shouted, totally ignoring his bleeding from the mouth, unconscious, lying in dung saturated straw girlfriend. A few seconds passed before he turned around and saw her on the ground. He put down the sledge-hammer and started running into the parking lot. Everybody just stood and stared as he got into his rusty, primer colored Monte Carlo with the mag tires and drove away, the spinning tires shooting up clumps of sod, dust and assorted stones into the evening summer sky. The girl was still on the ground and no one seemed to pay her much attention. It must not have been that big a deal since we and everyone else continued on the midway.

We saw a new ride that we hadn't seen in the past. Some sort of phony boat ride through a cave attraction. Being that this particular group of friends I associated with loved campy, ridiculous stuff, this looked kind of neat! An old, weathered building resembling a mill was the starting point of the ride. There was a big sign just before you walked up the steps to the ride platform:

"Ye Olde Mill of The Eternally Damned"

Be Very Afraid! The souls of the eternally damned reside here!! The demonic souls of very, very wicked individuals reside here and want nothing more than to kill you!! They relish at the opportunity to devour your flesh, chew on your bones and steal your soul!! They want to destroy you!! They want to erase your existence from this world and bring you into their realm of unimaginable horror!! Please no flash photography—this is somewhat irritating to the damned, evil spirits who are attempting to annihilate you!! Thank you!!

* You must be at least 6 inches tall to ride this attraction*

Pregnant women should not go on this ride unless they have a nota-rized doctor's note and have signed a waiver releasing the carnival and its employees from liability should the child be born with horns pro-truding from its head and have hooves instead of hands and feet

*You should not ride this attraction if you suffer from any of the following:
 - Heart ailments—Neck discomfort—Claustrophobia—Anorexia -
 - Jock itch—Osteoporosis—Malaria—Nervousness—Vertigo -
 - Hemorrhoids—Dandruff -

*You should avoid this ride if you are allergic to any of the following:
 - Super heated, toxic, diesel fumes—Mustard Gas—Paper—Linoleum—Massive Bee stings—Soy Ink -

Well, there wasn't a line for the attraction, so we decided to go on, even though my friend Patrick, suffered from dandruff. We climbed the few steps up to the platform and saw the "ride". It was an old, dented, aluminum canoe mounted on wooden, 2 x 4 stud axles with hard rubber lawn mower tires nailed to them. On the front, a massive chain—perhaps from the anchor of some large naval vessel— was hooked to the canoe with a bent coat hanger. On the back was a yellow flag with the image of the carnival's founder—Ezekiel M. Imacrabbage, a bald, mustached gentleman—silk-screened in black. And piping through the tinny speakers was that annoying noise from the Psycho shower scene mixed with moans and howls that one would hear around Halloween when some family on the street went and spent a few dollars to buy a recording of scary sounds that would scare the very young children and make the older ones laugh and come back with a supply of eggs and toilet tissue.

My friends and I looked at one another, shrugged, and decided, what the hell? So we walked up to the guy who was taking the tickets for the ride—who looked a whole lot like Bob Barker from the Price Is Right—handed him our tickets and climbed in to the wobbly contraption. We sat down on what appeared to be no more than a splintered, plywood plank, looking around for some sort of restraining devices. There were none. I asked the Bob Barker looking guy—with all those precautions on the sign outside, shouldn't there be some sort of seat belt, harness, heck, even a piece of rotted and frayed hemp weed rope or maybe an electrical extension cord we could manage to knot around our waists and lash ourselves to the decrepit vehicle? He looked at me with a big smile and said, "No."

He walked back to the lever that starts the ride and smiles at us again and says, "Don't forget to have your pets spayed and neutered. Even the fish, God dammit!" He started laughing and pulled the lever. The boat/car lurched forward and moved very slowly into the cavern entrance. It is pitch black inside as the vehicle moves ahead very slowly. After about 20 feet, we passed through black curtains and are right back outside to where we started the ride. That's it!? We all looked at each other and started talking rather loudly...

"What a lame ass ride!"

"Whose fuckin' idea was it to go on this fucking ride?"

"I want my fucking money back!"

"Anyone see my fucking bee sting kit?"

We just walked away grumbling and saw Bob waving to us and smiling. I yelled to him, "This ride sucks!"

"Yes, yes, it does," he replied, still smiling, "Come back soon, okay? And don't forget to visit our lovely gift shop! We're having a special on 'I Survived Ye Olde Mill of the Eternally Damned' T-shirts. Sure, they're all factory second, irregular products that don't fit properly—unless you have several dislocated joints and a few extraordinarily large growths— but what a bargain they are!!"

We turned away and headed down to midway, still grumbling a bit. We saw the Human Oddities attraction ahead and decided to go see that, forgetting about the horrible "ride" incident. We stood in front of the tented attraction and looked at the list, written in large black letters in script on a large, white board, of the freaks inside. There was guy who could stretch his arm like a rubber band. There was another who could eat light bulbs. There was a dwarf who could break dance really good. And there was one that was just called, "The Girl With Tools." And that show was about to start in a few minutes. We decided that we would go in.

We gave our tickets to a very large woman with a beard wearing a KISS muumuu and walked through the front curtains and into the ill-lit, musty smelling tent. The floor was the ground covered in smelly straw and sawdust. There were about 20 or so metal folding chairs facing the stage, which actually didn't look that bad—it looked like one from a dance hall saloon they always have in westerns. We took seats in the front and noticed that besides us, there were only six others. Then some peppy, loud, carnival music started playing as a gentleman came out wearing a plaid zoot suit with a polka dot tie who started yelling into a cardboard megaphone.

"Ladies and Gentlemen, Boys and Girls, Welcome to the show that will have you leaving here muttering, 'What the hell was that? How is it possible that a human being could do that? That was the most bizarre thing I have ever seen!' and 'Does anyone have a spare set of trousers and underwear, for I believe I soiled myself!' Yes, Ladies and Gentlemen, these are all human beings who, through some cruel twist of fate, have become oddities! Freaks! With features and abilities that will make any normal person suffer from severe bouts of gas and want to vomit from bewilderment! Be prepared to be stunned and amazed! For you will see things that go beyond the realms of credibility!!"

He paused here, I supposed, to wait to her some sort of applause or even a murmur of recognition from the few of us gathered. He heard nothing. He put the megaphone back up to his mouth and continued.

"Ladies and gentlemen, it is indeed a great thrill and it gives me great pleasure to introduce you to the featured attraction for this most amazing of evenings. Please, put your hands together for Sheila, the Girl With Tools!!"

We clapped as the music got louder and the curtain opened. Out from stage left came out a tall woman with a round face, long red hair and green eyes. She was wearing a very impressive red satin costume covered in silver and gold sequins and looked pleasing to the eye. She came to center stage and bowed. She walked to one side of the stage, then to the other, then back to center stage. We all were clapping and some of the other six individuals who were in attendance with us whistled, and one even shouted, "Take it off, baby! You know you want to!"

Sheila then proceeded towards a chair behind her that had a tool belt hanging from it. She smiled at us and put the tool belt around her slender waist. From stage right, two carnies rolled out something fairly big, draped in a red sheet. Sheila, still smiling at us, held her arms out to the side as if she were showing us a prize on a game show. She then walked to the side and pulled off the sheet. It was a framework of some sort. Sheila pulled out a hammer from her belt and turned to address the audience.

"This evening I will attempt to build a big dog house. I am building it for a gigantic, savage, animal that somewhat resembles a dog. He is my pet. Or at least he WAS my pet. My friend's boyfriend broke every bone in it's body simply because my pet was sniffing his crotch! Son—of — bitch! If I ever see him again, I'll kill the mother fucker!!"

She started beating the wooden framework with the hammer. She swung as hard as she could, but Sheila, being slender and exhibiting very little muscle tone—a weakling, could barely cause a dent in the soft pine woodwork. She collapsed on stage from fatigue after only several swings.

We all looked at each other as we stood up, ready to leave, when she called out from her prone position on the floor, "Sit the fuck down! You ain't seen my movie yet!"

Apparently, there was a movie with this attraction. In my hand was a yellow sheet of printed-paper stating that the exhibit included a short documentary on how Sheila ended up in the Ezekiel M. Imacrabbage Traveling Carnival. It also had a picture of that Bob Barker looking guy and a coupon for 2 cents off anything priced $75 or more at the "Ye Olde Mill of the Eternally Damned" gift shop. Well, I thought, at least the movie should be good.

Another curtain opened up on the stage revealing a very large, Movie Theater—sized screen. The lights went down on the tent (Sheila was still laying on the floor from exhaustion) and the movie began. A dancing cigarette came up on the screen and started talking.

"Everybody keeps telling you that smoking cigarettes is all bad. (Laughing) Well, you and I know better! Cigarette smoke is actually good! Scientific research and clinical tests have shown that cigarette smoke causes cancer and a slew of other very dangerous and lethal medical conditions in laboratory rats. And I don't know about you, but I hate rats—whether they live in a lab, in the sewers or in Chinese restaurants all over the world! I'm glad to hear that the blessed, smooth and oh so enjoyable smoke that emanates from glorious cigarettes causes them suffer so! Please sign the petition on the way out to pass the bill currently in Congress that will force every rat in the country to smoke unfiltered cigarettes! Thank you and enjoy the film!"

Some happy organ music began playing as the cigarette danced off and a big picture of Sheila appeared on the screen. She was smiling and had her watery eyes almost squinted shut due to the smoke from the cigarette, with a big ash, which was dangling from the corner of her mouth. Then a narrator (who sounded exactly like Robert Stack) began speaking as the picture remained up on the screen.

"What you are about to see is a documentary. Everything has been recreated, as no one knew who Sheila was before she came here and even if they did, I don't know who would want to follow her around with a movie camera to capture her life on celluloid. It just wouldn't be worth the time and effort."

(Some old, 8mm home movie scenes of a little baby and some grown-ups—perhaps her parents—are now up on the screen)

"Sheila, the Girl With Tools was born Sheilacca Buma Hoochahala on September 12, 1966 in Enid, Oklahoma to Ramon Elvis and Miriam Sweetwater Hoochahala. (A picture of a striking, dark hair, mustached and smiling Ramone is up on the screen) Ramone was a dance instructor who supplemented the family income by working part time for a manu-facturer of artificial flavorings—the type primarily used in ice cream and carbonated beverages—as the 'final stage tester.' Whenever Ramon wasn't teaching the tango, the chicken dance or two-step to the townsfolk, he was at the plant sampling the latest in artificial flavorings. Many believe that his overindulgence in "Choco-Coco"—the newly developed flavor-ing that tasted like chocolate and coconut—caused him to lose his mind. On February 27, 1971, Ramon Elvis Hoochahala left his only child and his wife to become a door-to-door vacuum cleaner salesman in Auckland, New Zealand. He was never heard from again."

(The image of Ramone fades and the picture of Miriam appears. She is smiling a big, too much lipstick smile, has pearls around her neck and is sporting a big bouffant hair-doo)

"Miriam, now left to tend for a child alone, and with no marketable skills, took a job as an instructor at the same dance studio where Ramon once worked. On her third day on the job, Miriam faked a fall during a beginner cha-cha lesson. She conspired with the local physician to claim that she had fractured several vertebrae in the fall and could no longer pursue gainful employment. She sued the dance studio and won. The dance studio had to close and Miriam never went to work again."

(A picture of Sheila—perhaps a seventh or eighth grade school photo—appeared on the screen. She was smiling broadly, showing her perfectly straight, immaculately white teeth and her hair meticulously styled.)

"Sheila was very popular during grade school and junior high. Whenever she was present she immediately became the center of atten-tion and the focus of every hormone driven, young man who she hap-pened to come across. Young men were constantly asking her out on dates but Miriam, being extremely strict with Sheila, refused any such notion until Sheila was at least a sophomore in High School. Sheila waited patiently for that time to come. It finally did."

(The screen now shows actors who are recreating the scenes and situations described by the narrator)

"Her Sophomore year of High School finally arrived, and Sheila was ecstatic!! Her mother released her reins a bit and allowed her daughter to go out with some of the boys that asked her out, but never on any car dates. Sheila wasn't totally overjoyed with this, but at least it was better than not going out at all. So far, all of her dates were little ones like going to the frozen milk fruit parlor or to the 'Spoiled Burro', the local burger joint. None were of any real significance or social importance in Sheila's eyes. She wanted to go somewhere nice where other people from her school could see how wonderful she really was. Like a dance.

"The Sophomore class had tried to throw a few dances in the cafeteria in the Fall and around Christmas but no one really wanted to dance and socialize in the same place where Agnes, the old, wrinkled, hair net wearing, lunch lady served the pathetic school lunches—no matter how much paper mache, streamers and balloons were stapled, glued and haphazardly thumb tacked to the wall.

"But in the spring the class planned to hold a dance at the Sunnyweed Country Club and Slightly Irregular and Damaged Office Supply Distribution Center, if they could raise enough money. The students all jumped at the chance to have a REAL dance, so they all went out and sold thousands of dollars of liquid soap and little wooden boxes that had two tea bags and a dried olive in it (and sold for $7.95 each) to friends, neighbors, relatives, and convicts at the state correctional institution. They had raised enough money to have their dance. Sheila was overjoyed!

"There was a nice young man by the name of Linus Jackson who asked Sheila to the Sophomore Dance and Arthritic Hawaiian Elephant Roast (The name of the affair was finally agreed to by a ballot. It beat out "The Sophomore Dance and Mentally Deranged Ethiopian Hippopotamus Slaughter" by one vote.). Sheila wanted to go with him and she ran home to ask her mother. It took a little arm bending, crying, screaming, and flat out begging, but her mother finally agreed.

"Miriam was very helpful in trying to find a dress for the event, even going to an old friend of the family who happened to be a seamstress to see if she could make something wonderful for her daughter. The family friend was somewhat senile, however, and instead of a prom dress, made a suit that was an exact duplicate of the one Neil Armstrong wore when he walked on the moon. They then went to the discount thrift store and bought something that at least resembled a dress or a burlap bag—it was a pretty close call either way—and Miriam managed to tailor it nicely using a stapler and iron—on denim patches.

"The night before the dance, Sheila couldn't sleep a wink. So she went into her mother's room and sat up with her, talking through the night and into the wee hours of the morning. Of course, the next morning Sheila was totally exhausted. She knew that she had to go to school that day or she would not be allowed to attend the dance. She drank several strong cups of espresso coffee loaded with sugar and went to school.

"During the bus ride she was alert and talkative with all her friends discussing the plans for the night ahead. However, when she was in homeroom, the hyper—stimulating effects of the extra strong coffee had worn off and she fell fast asleep right after the salute to the flag. She was in such a deep sleep, the teacher couldn't wake her and she had to be carried by several of her classmates to the nurse's office. The nurse tried to bring her to by using smelling salts, slapping her repeatedly across the face, jabbing her with a needle, and repeatedly shocking her with the split, frayed ends of an extension cord that was plugged in, but none of those methods worked. When Sheila did finally wake up, it was time to go home. Miriam had heard of what happened at school and spent the remainder of the afternoon with Sheila baking her Grandma Fifi's amazing garlic and habanera cookies and making frozen Hamisicles until it was time to get dressed for the dance.

"Linus Jackson had just got his drivers license the day before and was ever so happy that he would be allowed to drive Sheila to the dance. As a matter of fact, Linus' parents were going to allow him to take the family station wagon that was 15 years old and looked absolutely immaculate. Linus was excited as he went to pick up his rented tuxedo with black vinyl shoes—with the built in lifters that made him look 3 inches taller—at Schleppy's Formal Wear and Off Track Betting Parlor. So excited that he forgot to apply the parking brake or put the vehicle in gear before he went in. When Linus came out, he didn't see the family treasure parked where he left it, but he did somehow manage to glimpse out of the corner of his eye a tremendous fireball shooting flames and super heated gasses into the humid Oklahoma sky.

"Apparently the family heirloom rolled down the slight incline of the street, hit a fully loaded gasoline tanker truck and exploded. He called Sheila, and without going into much detail, said that he would not have the pleasure of accompanying her to the event that evening. He then packed his belongings and headed off to the juvenile correctional facility where his parents insisted he go.

"Well, Miriam took this to be an omen of some sort and didn't allow Sheila to go to another big social event—though she did manage to get in a few dates at the bowling alley and even once went to the 'Chitty Chitty Bang Bang' death cage wrestling match—until the next year when the Junior Prom took place.

"That year, Alonzo McFlaherty, the alternate co-captain of the school's ice sculpting team, asked her to go with him and Sheila couldn't wait! She and her mother brought out the pink chiffon dress from last year and after some minor alterations—the removal of several rusted and bent staples—Sheila completely put last year's fiasco out of her mind and was set on having a wonderful time.

"About ten minutes or so before Alonzo was supposed to come and pick Sheila up, the phone rang. It was Alonzo's mother. She said that Alonzo was at the hospital having his stomach pumped after he swallowed a 48-ounce bottle of Jean Nate perfume in an attempt to battle a chronic bout of halitosis. The doctors said that he will be fine physically but insisted that he be placed under observation in the Psychologically Unstable and Probably Just Plain Crazy ward. Sheila thought briefly about going stag, but besides Miriam telling her that no self respecting mother—even one that commits insurance fraud and lies under oath to get out of working the rest of her life—would have her daughter do so, she felt that she wouldn't enjoy herself. So she went to bed at seven.

"Miriam, again, would not let Sheila attend any function until the next year. Sheila did manage to trick her mother and met some young man at the Combine and Other Field Equipment Demolition Derby, but that turned out to be quite a disappointment. Her date's father came down to the event, grabbed him by the ear and took him home, screaming at him the whole way. The boy had entered his father's brand new, $250,000 multi-thrasher combine in the event, hoping to win a couple of last row seats to the Bay City Roller Reunion Tour. The scrap alone was now worth about $250—and that's if the scrap dealer was drunk.

"So Sheila waited a whole year until the Senior Prom came around and prayed that nothing would go wrong this time. She thought on several occasions that she was on the verge of a nervous breakdown—breaking out in hives, developing severe instances of post-nasal drip—but managed to keep her inferiority complex in check. Travis Cronstaff, captain of the school's Gambling and Prostitution team, asked her to go with him to the Senior Prom and Semi—Inflated, Highly Toxic Hydrogen Balloon Race. Sheila said yes, after checking with Miriam, who also hoped to hell that nothing would go wrong this year.

"This was Sheila's last chance to attend a major school function—well except for graduation, but she didn't care about that—and hopefully nothing was going to prevent her from going. The day before the event, the telephone rang and Miriam answered it. After a few seconds of silence, Miriam's face fell."

"Don't even tell me!" cried Sheila, "I'm not going to the Senior Prom tomorrow night!"

"No, that's not it," sobbed Miriam, "My 125 year old great Aunt Bethusula was killed by a bus while walking her pet Jamaican Wild Jackass and I have to go and pay my respects."

"Whew! Is that it?! I thought I wouldn't be able to go to the Prom tomorrow night!!" shrieked Sheila.

"Well, I'll be leaving tonight and I will be gone for a couple of days. I hope that you can handle everything yourself, and I really hope you enjoy yourself tomorrow night."

"Mom, you don't have to worry about a thing," said Sheila with a sweet smile on her face.

"After a bunch of hugs and kisses and going over an extensive list of things to do—which Sheila promptly threw in the wastebasket as soon as her mother left—Miriam took off for Hays, Kansas (Once voted the town one would like to go to if they should happen to die while choking on pulled pork—from a survey done on American towns by Mercenary Magazine), where her family was from.

"Sheila was getting very excited about the Prom. 'This is gonna be great!' she kept telling herself, sometimes out loud. This was it, the last chance, and she was finally going to do it! The Supreme; The Senior Prom and Semi—Inflated, Highly Toxic Hydrogen Balloon Race! Sheila was getting TOO excited. So much so that she began sweating profusely from every pore in her body."

"I'll never be able to get to sleep," she told herself, "But I have to or I'll get those horrible bags under my eyes, you know, the ones that no amount of base or makeup will ever hide! I've must relax! I've got it!"

"Sheila ran into her mother's room and ransacked through her personal possessions until she came upon what she was seeking; Miriam's sleeping pills. 'If I take a few of these, I'll be thoroughly refreshed come tomorrow!' So at about 8 pm, Sheila, totally disregarding the dosage information, red warning labels and the synthetic voice warning 'Please read the directions' accompanied by miniature sirens and flashing lights on the bottle of pills, took seven sleeping pills after finally deciphering the complex numerical code required to deactivate the child-proof cap. Then she went to sleep.

"The Prom invaded Sheila's dreams. All she could think about was Travis and the Prom. She pictured him in his white tuxedo and green, metal tipped, frog skin cowboy boots, pulling up to the house in his father's Orange Mercedes. She saw herself floating towards the car on Travis' arm. The rest of his body caught up with them at the car. She got into the car, Travis holding the door open for her like a perfect gentleman that he was.

"They headed to the restaurant, chatting and laughing the whole way, where they were meeting several other couples for dinner. They all sat around eating lobster, crab cakes and other creatures that only just yesterday were living a life of leisure in the sea. They talked about the fun time ahead before heading back out to the car. They arrived right on time at Flomongo's Partially Covered Convention Hall and High-Powered Rifle Range, where the event was to be held.

"Inside was a magnificent ballroom with glittering lights. Everyone was sort of milling around the liquefied crayon punch table waiting for the photographer to take pictures. Then the band came on. Everyone headed to the dance floor when Mega Decibel, the loudest Prom, Bar Mitzvah and Wedding band in the world—banned from every county fair in the country because they really annoyed the carnies—took the stage.

"After a few catchy, unbelievably loud, dance tunes which blew several gaping holes in the partial ceiling, they slowed down the pace with a romantic melody that was so loud it turned the half and half containers on the tables into little wheels of aged cheddar cheese. From nowhere an eye searing lime-green laser light focused it's powerful beam on Travis and Sheila. They embraced each other tightly and Travis shouted lovingly into her ear as loud as he could, 'Oh Sheila, Sheila…'"

"Sheila…Sheila, wake up honey," said Miriam as she shook Sheila back into a semi-lucid state.

"Mom! What are you doing home? Did you forget something? I thought you were going to see your family," said Sheila, groggily.

"I did, Sheila. That was three days ago."

"Three days ago!?," screamed Sheila, "I must have slept for three days! I missed the Prom!"

"Sheila dropped out of school the following Monday, only three weeks from her High School graduation. She was inconsolable. She would have fits of rage and start screaming obscenities at her mother and strangers on street corners as they were waiting for busses and taxis.

"She began roaming the streets and back alleys of Enid dressed in filthy, tattered clothing. She refused to bathe regularly and smelled bad most of the time. She found a stray animal, which if you were drunk and squinted real hard or suffered from acute cataracts, resembled a dog and made it her companion.

"Sheila managed to find work, although she never held a job for more than three days. She once took a position with a car rental company but was fired after two days when it was discovered that Sheila was selling the cars to Colombian Nationals for corn powder cigarettes and shattered cow bones which she would use to make some sort of bizarre voodoo charm by sticking the shards of bone into rotting oranges and selling them on street corners to tourists, prostitutes and former convicts who had to come to Enid, Oklahoma to clean the streets and statues of pigeon and other assorted birds' droppings as part of their community service.

"She also worked for 7 hours and 36 minutes as a spackler at a new home construction site. She was fired when she was caught selling the barrels of spackling compound to Colombian Nationals for corn powder cigarettes and shattered cow bones.

"Sheila worked a total of 18 hours and 17 minutes for the manufacturer of little cars that circus clowns drive in (the ones that hold up to 25 clowns, 47 dwarfs or two African elephants) as the girl who brought rotten egg salad sandwiches, scalding wheat beer, and unfiltered celery seed cigarettes to the barely literate and highly unskilled, illegal immigrants who painstakingly and with great pride glued together the flimsy vehicles with an adhesive made from honey and flavored oatmeal.

"On her second day on the job, Sheila was asked to deliver one of the fabulous and wonderfully funny vehicles (evidently they were not aware of Sheila's habit of pilfering company property and her fondness of corn powder cigarettes and shattered cow bones) to the Ezekiel M. Imacrabbage Traveling Carnival and Lawn Mower Blade Sharpener Emporium. (Ezekiel dropped the blade sharpener emporium after selling only one sharpener in twenty years—and that was to an 85 year old, cataracted heroin freak, who was convinced by Ezekiel, using some sort of parlor-room, trick hypnosis and hallucinogens, that it was a frozen yogurt machine).

"Sheila attempted to sell the minuscule vehicle to the Colombian Nationals, but the Nationals—who have in the past purchased from Sheila such things as defective toothpaste tubes (they had caps on both ends), bags of sawdust, ice and giant vats of Mama Beratelli's Old Fashioned Nacho Cheese Flavored Cake and Brownie Icing—refused to purchase the vehicle, claiming that they had a 'reputation to keep'. Sheila decided to take the vehicle to the carnival. She had found her home...

"And now she's probably passed out in the floor in front of you..."

The movie just ended, no credits no music, just blank screen. The lights came up and the guy with the cardboard megaphone came back out—Sheila was still lying on the floor of the stage—and shouted, "Alright now, get the hell out! Move it! Do I need the police?! Let's move it!! Okay, that's it! Will somebody please call the cops!!" We ran to the slit in the tent fabric and left the attraction. But instead of being let out into the midway, we were in a bar. They were in the middle of the "Beat

Your Liver" promotion. All drinks were 12 cents between 5 and 5:13 pm. You could drink as much as you wanted to, but you couldn't order another drink until you finished the one you had. People were at the bar pounding down shots of premium liquor one right after the other. At 5:13:01 pm the Bob Barker looking guy from the crappy ride blew a whistle and made an announcement.

"Okay, folks, let's quiet down a bit!! I know you are all probably so freaking drunk you don't know what I'm saying, or you're probably not even able to see me…but it's time to announce the winner of the life-time pass to the Wonderful World of Salt Water Taffy Museum and the Monroeville 'We've Had Only One Potentially Life Eradicating Accident—This Week' Nuclear Power Plant!! And the winner, having poured down his gullet 6 shots of tequila, 3 shots of vodka, 4 shots of rye, 2 shots of grain alcohol, 3 bottles of malt liquor, and a big mug of water with the liquid cleaning additive they use to sanitize the glassware is…Ezekiel M Imacrabbage!!"

He then began ringing this brass bell behind the bar…which turned into the annoying beeping sound that my cheapy alarm clock emits every morning, reminding me that it's time to get up and start yet another long, drowsy and feeling ill day of research. And this dream was all due to a massive fried appetizer munching spree—fried Mozzarella sticks, fried Onion Rings, fried Calmer, fried Oysters, fried Southwestern Egg rolls (Like an regular egg roll except that inside is refried beans, some seaweed—like substance and chili powder), fried Chicken Wings (smothered in some sauce that made my fingernails fall off)—followed by ten or so of "Mega Malt 500" malt liquors–"The Only Malt Liquor That Dares to Use Volatile and Potentially Life Threatening Ingredients."

* * * * * * * * * * * * * * * * *

Once, around the Christmas Holiday, I decided to make myself another bizarre sandwich "creation" and let its mind altering effects take place in my head. Sometimes the correct combination of foods will react with each other producing effects similar to experimental, government issued LSD. This particular night I made myself a bacon, lettuce, tomato, cheese, sardine, duck fat, mustard seed, tripe, codfish, meatball and horseradish hoagie. I swallowed it all down with a piping hot bowl of Yugoslavian coffee (the kind that permanently colors your esophagus and adenoids a dark black) with Parmesan cheese and six, twice refined and triple bleached sugar packets. I figured that this would take my mind off the horrendous task of Christmas shopping, especially since I had no money. It did the trick.

I went upstairs and attempted to sleep after guzzling down a gallon and a half of a generic, pseudo—Pepto Bismol product (available at all those nifty bulk shopping places. Really neat places to shop, they are. I'm still using the 75 pound Brut deodorant stick and 475 ounce, mega—tube of "Old Doc McIntyre the Animal Chiropractor's " tooth abrasive I purchased in 1979 to this day!), to help ease the massive cramping, extreme bloating and possibly quiet down the very audible moaning and deafening gurgling sounds in my gastrointestinal tract. After spending several long minutes tossing and turning trying to get into a comfortable position in order to get to some shut- eye, I decided that sleeping in a sitting—up position with my back against the wall proved to be the least painful. Unfortunately, the way my chin rested upon my chest effectively cut off my breathing mechanism (and nearly dislocated my skull from my spine) causing me to pass out and roll onto the floor where I spent the remainder of the night in a convoluted fetal position—and where I had my dream. Though I have never really made any attempts to try to interpret my dreams nor try to relate them to real life experiences, I tend to believe that this one manifested itself directly from my fears about holiday shopping…I think.

In the dream I went out to the mailbox and picked up a whole bunch of bills and junk mail and one large envelope marked "The StrangeCo Shopping Guide." I tried to figure out where I had ever seen any of the StrangeCo stores, but none came to mind. Probably one of those lame, shop at home catalogs that showcased such neat items like a liquid that dissolves tree stumps, magnifying pill cutters or anti—embolism stockings ("the stretch nylon/spandex massages arthritic and varicose vein discomfort") everybody was getting into, I thought. I was genuinely hoping it would be one of those surplus store catalogs where you could buy a used navy bomber jacket with shrapnel embedded into the lining (cool) or the turret of a partially destroyed monster tank, complete with massive 75mm cannon (really cool) so I rushed inside to take a look.

Once inside I put all the junk mail (including an offer to have my haircut at the local barber school—located inside Graterford State Penitentiary—for a quarter and a pack of cigarettes) into a nice neat pile and threw all the bills, unopened, into the fireplace—which, incidentally, I do in real life. I opened the big envelope and removed the glossy, multi-colored catalog. I turned a few pages and was captivated. I went to the sofa, sat down and began perusing the pages. What a neat catalog! Just imagine great pictures in terrific color (remember the Sears catalog...yeah, well, this was like a million times better looking than their great Christmas edition) with corresponding descriptions. I turned towards the middle of the catalog and saw...

Stationary:

StrangeCo's famous "Dante's Inferno" pen: Are you tired of watching that special someone seemingly waste away their precious life moments by constantly writing? You know, a little note here, a boring letter to their loved ones there, an attempt to write a novel in a little notebook they always carry around with them right over there. Well, this is the gift they simply have to have! This specially engineered writing apparatus was designed to give that writer something "hot" to write about! The StrangeCo scientists have developed a method in which the salts and oils of the human skin will cause the casing of the pen to react somewhat like a road flare, shooting a 4500 degree flame 8—12 feet (actual height will vary depending upon wind conditions and barometric pressure) into the air! Now that special someone will able to enjoy life to its fullest—right after he or she gets out of the burn trauma center of the hospital!.................package of 3 single use pens................$37.63

StrangeCo's "Glu-Nothing" glue: It looks like glue, it smells like glue (sniff it enough and you'll be smacked out of your mind, dancing around your house like fairy in tight, pointy shoes for up to 48 hours!), but it has one major difference—it NEVER hardens! Watch as your friends start ripping the hair out of their heads as it'll take them forever to glue simple things together. Watch as their frustration mounts as even gluing pieces of onion—skin paper together becomes a virtual impossibility! Great for those God—awful projects that you never want to finish!....................................473 oz. tube..............$13.09

StrangeCo "Quick Draw" High-Powered Staple Gun: Not only does this fabulous piece of stationary have the power to staple cinder blocks to granite boulders, you can use it to protect your home from intruders! Our finest .45 caliber staple gun provides clean, easy, accurate shots time after time. Powerful too! The staples have been designed to pierce armor plating up to 1/4 inch thick! And you don't need any type of training or even a permit to carry a staple gun! Also available with a genuine iguana skin holster
......................staple gun with 550 rounds of staples......$231.17
......................genuine iguana skin holster..................$29.15
......................Box of 812 rounds of staples...............$63.23

StrangeCo "Dissolvo!" Disintegrating Paper: Another fantastic product from the StrangeCo laboratories! A great joke to play on a friend. Let your college buddy—you know, the one who has been in school forever—type or print their doctorate thesis or term papers on these ordinary looking sheets of paper. Then hold on and get ready to laugh! Our scientists have discovered away to rapidly increase the decomposing process of wood and paper products (make sure you check out our spectacular "No Weather" deck and patio furniture!!). After 48hrs of being unwrapped and exposed to the earth's atmosphere, that once pristine looking paper will be nothing but dust! Imagine the look of horror and surprise as your college pal turns in what he thinks is hundreds of hours of work, but in reality is nothing more than a folder full of what looks like cigar ashes! Tears of laughter will roll down your cheek as you watch him try to stammer out any excuse or a possible explanation. "Well, I..no really, I spent two days just writing it…please, something very horrible has happened here! Oh shit!" Feel your sides split with laughter as he drops out of college and joins the Peace Corps or the Postal Service!………………………One (1) ream of hermetically sealed paper…………………………………$17.63

I scanned through the rest of the stationary section to see what other cool stuff they had…

StrangeCo Designer Broken Pencils:…Gucci, Klein and other designers put their art to work on these pencils of the eighties. Send a swatch of your suit or dress material and we'll try our hardest to match the pencil to your wardrobe!! Send in a piece of a man's polyester suit or stretch pants for women, and you'll receive a letter signed by all the designers stating that you have absolutely have no taste you shouldn't be writing with colored chalk, charcoal, or crayons let alone one of their damaged, yet highly stylish, pencils! Suitable for framing!!

StrangeCo High-Pressure Fountain Pens.... Spews out the entire ink cartridge like a poorly tapped beer keg just as you're about to sign the mortgage papers or endorse that lottery check! Please use in well-ventilated areas and keep away from open flames!!

StrangeCo "Cheat and Chew" Edible Cheat Sheets: Write the answers to the big test that you managed to pilfer from the professor's desk on this paper and then chew it to get rid of the evidence. Contains 25% of the RDA of vitamin G and riboflavin. Available in a delicious grapefruit and watercress flavor!!

StrangeCo Symptom Pills:...Appear to come down with something so terrible and vile that you don't have to go to class or go to work!! Available in the following diseases:

Leprosy, Tuberculosis, Hepatitis, Gigantism, Stroke, Incurable Gout, Bubonic Plague and Dengue Fever (Bone Breaking Fever).

And, as an added bonus, we will provide you with a years supply of phony doctor's notes stating that you have been miraculously cured and are now able to return to work without any risk of infecting your co—workers. Also comes with a surgical mask that you can wear around the office—for either when you're preparing to get sick (" I really don't want you all to be exposed to these deadly germs I am harboring! I would hate for them to have to quarantine us here!"), or for when you have just returned (" I am really feeling so much better!! The guys at the Center for Disease Control just told me to wear this mask around the place, for, you know, 'Just in case' as they put it! Hey, is that my spoon you're eating that yogurt with?").

StrangeCo Impressive Book Binders...Fool and bamboozle teachers, bosses, friends and loved ones with these fantastic bookbinders. They'll think you are reading something really good, when in fact your ogling a collection of poorly written porn stories or a copy of Dianetics! Choose from any of the following titles:

War and Peace, Moby Dick, The Communist Manifesto, The History of the World, The 1984 Physicians Desk Reference, The StrangeCo Winter/Spring Fashion Catalog, The Reader's Digest Condensed Version of The Dead Sea Scrolls.

I turned a few pages ahead to see a really cool section....

Sporting Goods:

StrangeCo "Stand Firm" Golf Shoes: Our unique, patented golf footwear (the term "shoes" really doesn't do them justice) give you the steady stance you need to swing for the long ball! Each shoe has 57 cleats—each an amazing 5 1/2 inches long! And with their super dense lead soles (the same type used to keep the astronauts from floating off the moon and heading off to the sun to be roasted alive), you can virtu-ally stand sideways in a sand trap during a hurricane with these babies on! Also know as the "Monster Shoe," because of it's uncanny resem-blance to the type of shoe Frankenstein (actually more like Herman Munster) used to wear, you'll stand head and shoulders above your golf-ing buddies!! Comes with a 3 speed, synchro—mesh, motorized pulley system that attaches to your legs to make it easy to walk!! Just don't for-get to take them off before hitting the 19th hole or you will cause thou-sands of dollars in damages to the floor and carpeting!!...........Sizes 5 and 10 7/8EEE only......................$63.57

StrangeCo "What the Hell?" Golf Balls: When you need to hit that straight shot.... this is NOT the ball you want! But you'll definitely want your golfing buddies to use it! StrangeCo scientists have discovered a way to incorporate defective, Hungarian submarine gyroscopes into these seemingly normal looking golf balls guaranteeing that the game will never be the same again! Watch as the ball wobbles around the green, doing figure eights and other crazy patterns before rolling a good 45 yards from the green with just the slightest of touches! And watch out for those drives. This ball has been known to turn the slightest of slices into dangerous flight patterns for a speeding projectile that will smack you in the back of your own head! Comes with a flack jacket and protective headgear. Optional tracking system can help you find the ones that "got away" for up to three miles and from under 123 feet of water! Watch as your friends sit there with their jaws dropping muttering "What the hell...?"..................Sleeve of 3 golf balls.................................$35.87.........With built in tracking device to locate lost balls.......................$35.88

StrangeCo "Smokin'!" Golf Cart: Burn up the fairways...literally! StrangeCo engineers have spent thousands of man hours and millions of dollars of crucial Federal and State grant money previously targeted for the "Lunch for Those Not Really That Hungry Now, Thank you" government program to develop, for the true golf enthusiast, the ultimate joyride for the golf course! We have combined the low-key, modest styling of your average golf cart with the incredible thrust of a 575 horsepower alcohol burning funny car engine! This amazing vehicle has been clocked doing 247mph on the long 17th at Bermuda Hills Golf Course and Permanent Hair Removal Center—without totally disintegrating like our previous test models! The intentionally designed defective front end and prehistoric braking system (the same type that was banned from stagecoaches in 1883 for their lack of even being able to slow the wooden vehicles with exceptionally large wheels from rolling backward on a 2% incline—except ours look nicer!) will make every game you play with this cart seem like your last! Comes with a waiver stating, essentially, that if you act like a jackass and kill yourself or others, we will bear no responsibility and will disavow any knowledge of your existence or having ever purchased anything from us. Also comes with 45 minute (Very, very) Limited Warranty.

Scanning down, I noticed all the really cool stuff they had in the sporting area...

StrangeCo Shrinking Jock Straps.... Special materials and secret manufacturing techniques make these babies shrink to half their original size at the mere hint of sweat. Used by the Vienna "Older Men Who Sound a Little Bit Like " Boys Choir to ensure their ability to consistently reach those really high notes!!

StrangeCo "Super Ball"...Our famous 57 1/4lb bowling ball made from the finest highly polished granite. Show them who the king of the lanes really is! Specially designed, minuscule, high voltage electromagnets embedded into the glove/arm brace mechanism allow you to handle the ball with ease as the opposing ion—charged fields that are created allows the ball to virtually "float" when it is your hand! Please avoid water—that includes excessive sweating!!—in order to avoid massive electrocution!

StrangeCo Referee Whistle Amplifier...With this amazing little device, you no longer have to worry about being heard over a stadium full of drunken Irish soccer fans screaming poorly written fight songs and assorted other obscenities ever again!!! As a matter of fact, everyone will immediately quiet down as they notice blood trickling from their ears!! Another breakthrough in micro-audio technology has given us the necessary tools to develop an amplifying system that produces sounds in the decibel range similar to one holding a stethoscope up to a Saturn V rocket before take off!! Caution: Has been known to make dogs' eyes roll back into their heads and suffer occasional cranial combustion.

StrangeCo Thermo—Nuclear, Heat Seeking Javelin... Just aim it a point far away (very far away) and throw it. Mere moments after your release, the built in, reusable, solid—fuel rocket boosters help it go just a little bit farther!! It'll go incredibly far—but run for cover because the subsequent explosion will destroy 2 1/2 square miles! Comes with a Turkish government issued (and twice recalled) radiation suit and a pair of dark sunglasses designed for children.

StrangeCo Serrated Ice Skates... You'll never see these things in Olympic competition (although, you might see them worn by skaters in some low quality ice shows usually held in some sloppily built rinks at flea markets throughout the South) since these skates will cause tremendous grooves and valleys in the ice—that only you will be able to handle! Be hailed as the "King or Queen of the Rink" as after only two or three times around, you will be the only one able to still skate!! Talk about serendipity!! While working hard to develop a one season, steel belted snow tire with mechanically retractable, cotton—reinforced tin studs, one of our engineers, during an aroma—therapy session gone awry, stumbled across an idea of crossing a serrated vegetable peeler with an ice-skate!! The result? An absolutely amazing product that allows you to glide with ease across frozen surfaces while leaving an impassable trail of scarred, ravaged and deeply grooved rink surface in your wake!! Please avoid pond skating with these, okay?

StrangeCo Lead Reinforced Boxing Gloves.. It's okay! You just keep using that Soloflex as a clothes hanger! Go down to the local pugilists' club and knock down the champ (and probably break his jaw, too!) in only one punch! No matter how much weight lifting he did or street style fighting with sharpened kitchen utensils as weapons he experienced while he was serving time in the state pen for aggravated assault with intent to kill, he will not be prepared for the can of "whoop ass" you're going to lay on him!! The specially coated lead alloy built into the gloves avoids detection from any type of metal finding device.

StrangeCo Inflatable Yachts.. How would you like to look like a dignified human being rather than the white trailer trash that you are? Well, we can't help with everything, but we do try! Look like a snob tooling around the waterways with our famous 150ft inflatable yachts! Made of a slightly durable (it has been known to stay together, on several occasions, while the packaging is removed) polyplastapaper compound, this fantastic toy of the rich will provide you with hours (and we do mean only hours—like 5 or 6—that's it) of living out your fantasies!! Just open up the package, put in 5 1/2 tons of sand in the liner for ballast, and then start blowing!! We recommend using a pump since you would tear your diaphragm, collapse your lungs and probably die before blowing it up by mouth!!

StrangeCo Flammable Canoes… Whether you know an old friend who passed away and wanted to be roasted upon the waters like the Vikings used to do or that crazy Aunt Matilda (the former circus freak that not even carnie folk and gypsies would associate with) insists on going camping with you and your family, we have what you want!! By improving upon the technology developed during WWII for underwater corrosives and explosives, we were able to make this fantastic flammable flotation device!! When 50 ft or deeper of water is under the craft, highly sensitive and powerful incendiary detonators are activated, causing the rather innocuous looking watercraft (modeled after the canoes that Lewis and Clark used to keep in reserves if ever their good canoes failed) to erupt into a raging inferno within a matter of seconds!!

StrangeCo Dissolvable Camping Equipment… This top of the line gear (tents, sleeping bags, cots and designer outerwear for the fashionable camper) dissolves when it comes in contact with rain, dew, or even drool!

*StrangeCo "Super Eyes" Magnifying Ski Goggles…*These marvels of optical enhancement experimentation are finally available for humans!! Previously used to help blind as bats moles see better, these babies will magnify your field of vision over 1000 times! Try attacking the slopes with these on!! Is that a majestic and magnificent Redwood tree in front of you? Nope. It's merely a dirty and slightly splintered Popsicle stick some youngster stuck into the ground!! Imagine the fun and excitement you'll have next time you strap on those skis or snowboard!! But, please, don't look directly at the sun or you eyes will boil and burst!

All this stuff seemed so damn cool and I wondered why I had never seen any of this stuff around before! I jumped ahead to…

Home Appliances:

StrangeCo Anti-Aircraft Toaster…..We've combined the fine art of making toast with the fine art of warfare! This wonderful device makes toast perfect every time! And with one flick of a switch, you'll be able to shoot your finely toasted garlic bagel (ready for strawberry cream cheese) or pumpernickel slice in speeds of excess of 800mph, knocking down enemy aircraft with uncanny accuracy!…………………$4765.19

*StrangeCo "HurriClean" Bathroom Fan…*We have taken old world craftsmanship and just tossed it out the freaking window in refurbishing these monstrously huge Boeing 747 jet turbine engines into magnificently effective bathroom fans! Guaranteed to rid your bathroom of any unwanted, unpleasant odors that might cause someone to wretch. Never leave your bathroom smelling like a couple of filthy and deranged weasels climbed into your walls and died again!! Also has been known to drastically reduce levels of breathable oxygen in house, lower barometric air pressures, and cause occasional home implosions! This massive air cleaning system runs on an optional, specially designed self—generating, super efficient power plant available for $2,500—or you can simply stick two copper pennies into a lemon and run some old speaker wires to it. Comes with an easy to install (if you're a master mechanic that has a lot of experience with ratio calibrations, torque requirements, schematic reading, and loads of experience in troubleshooting) seat belt kit for the toilet so you don't get sucked into the razor sharp turbines!!..$16,132.77

StrangeCo "Presto"...An absolutely ingenious home product created by our very special engineers. By expounding upon the ideas and theories of Enrico Fermi and former scientists from the Manhattan Project and by consulting with the master craftsmen of several, very large, infant bathing devices manufacturers, we have developed the world's first thermonuclear pressure cooker that will make soups, stews and tough as jackass leather cuts of meats the best they can be in a matter of seconds! And with one little adjustment (requiring two Phillips head screwdrivers, a tire iron, a 45 ft roll of copper wire, a quart of spackle and a safety pin), it doubles as a baby bassinet! The perfect gift for the mother to be or for anyone who likes to make barely digestible, 15 days past expiration date meats taste somewhat acceptable (if one suffers from severely damaged taste buds)...........................$571.09

Scanning through the section...

StrangeCo "Hell Point" ovens...Ever wonder what makes the sun so damn hot? Well, we managed to recreate the fusion method that takes place at the sun's core and packaged it into a home friendly device (If your home is made of solid granite—even then, eh, a bit iffy) that reaches temperatures exceeding 3500 degrees Celsius...faster than a microwave!

StrangeCo 75h.p. Diesel Powered Carving Knife...(and the smaller 15h.p. steak knives) Make those holiday meals oh so much more memorable when it only takes you less than 35 seconds to carve an entire cow. Cuts through bones like butter. Comes with adjustable table gauges so you don't inadvertently slice your cherry wood table or marble countertops like a slab of soft cheese.

StrangeCo "Eski-Cool" Air Conditioners...Specifically designed for...well, for nothing, actually. Nothing has ever had to be this cold before!! But, since we already developed it and have a few on hand, we decided to market it as an "extreme" cooling device for places where it gets really hot—like the planet Mercury. These monstrosities create 300,000,000 BTUs of cooling power and can make it snow like it does in the Himalayas! Ever see those science shows where they put a hammer into liquid nitrogen then break the hammer? Well, this will freeze the liquid nitrogen until it just dries into a misty powder and blows away!

StrangeCo "Hurray!" Smoke Detectors...Smoke Detectors and such have always relied on shrieking whistles or blaring sirens to warn you of impending doom. Well, we at StrangeCo have taken our special detection devices to another, more sane level. Instead of a Massive Foghorn belting out incredible decibel levels (please see the StrangeCo "It's Done Already" 3 minute egg timer), we have developed a perfect little product that emits a pleasant bird chirping sound when the fire is out, the temperature of the charred flooring has cooled down to less than 135 degrees and only an acceptable amount (determined by Jackie, the guy who solders stuff for our corporation) of deadly, carbon gases remain. Much less nerve racking, wouldn't you say? We would!

StrangeCo "Dynamo" Toothbrush...Dental diseases and Horrendous disorders of the gums prove to be on the rise. Well, it doesn't take a scientist to see that it's because we eat tons of crap a year and just plain ole neglect our teeth. But it does take a scientist, a StrangeCo scientist at that, to see the need for the most effective cleaning devices ever invented for the mouth. By utilizing the technology (and a lot of the parts) that run the engines on those gigantic trucks they use to haul boulders and have tires bigger than a four-story house and by incorporating bristles that closely resemble a paint stripper attachment you put on a high-speed drill, we have done it!! Our mega—hydraulic, piston powered, nitro—infused, gasoline-fueled teeth cleaner provides you with the strength necessary to demolish any plaque (and some of the smaller, more fragile teeth in your head) and scare the hell out of any bacteria!! YOU WILL NEVER SUFFER FROM PLAQUE AGAIN…though the carbon monoxide may cause varying levels of brain damage or flat out kill you! Please brush responsibly and always wear a portable air supply!!

I was having a blast browsing through this catalog! I got to a special section that was all in yellow in the back that had a disclaimer written on the front sheet of the section….

"All of the items listed previously in our fantastic catalog are for 'normal' people. But there are those whom we know among us, that are less intelligent, less civilized and less…well, just less than the rest of us. We know them as BUFFOONS. If you know any BUFFOONS and wish to purchase a gift for them, but in the name of God and all that's holy why you would, here are a few suggestions…"

For BUFFOONS only:

StrangeCo's BUFFOONICK'S Cube…Almost the same as the hot selling "Rubik's Cube", but much easier…all the sides are the same color! And all the sides are glued together…essentially a colored cube, similar to what a small child would play with before their eyes are really able to function properly. Comes with an instruction guide, but, really, it's not necessary to have one. We don't know why one would want to buy this..$13.41

StrangeCo's BUFFinky.... Just like the ever-popular "Slinky" except this one attacks small pets and strangles them! StrangeCo scientists from the Biomedical—Mechanical Division stumbled onto one of their greatest inventions to date...and it's a toy!! An incredible combination of metal, muscle from a burro's hind leg and a AAA battery source! This incredible discovery/toy actually walks UP stairs!! Hell, if these guys spent more time working and less time slacking off and drinking triple mocha lattes, they could have the BUFFinky driving the family sedan!!..............BUFFinky w/defective carrying case/cage...$26.09

StrangeCo BUFFOONa Hoop...Remember that old classic, the "Hoola Hoop"? Well, you can forget it, because this is entirely different. Instead of always relying upon our incredible staff of highly educated and specially trained engineers and scientific personnel, we asked our janitorial and cafeteria people to design and put together a toy. It was for BUF-FOONS, we had our interpreter explain to them, so quality wasn't so much a concern. After much screaming and yelling, waving dead chickens and meat cleavers, the group came through. Manufactured from the remains of mangled hang-gliders, this is triangular with bits of sharp aluminum sticking out. If you can actually get it to swing around your waist, it may saw you in half!..................$00.57

StrangeCo BUFFOONopoly...What happens when you put a little "mental expander" (please see page 7756, "Fun Powders and Crazy Concoctions") powder into the drinks of the specialists in the StrangeCo Game Division? This is what. A hideously distorted version of that old classic, "Monopoly." There are only two properties and you must own them both to build houses. There are 42 "Take a Chance, Punk, I Friggin'

Dare You!!" Spaces, 4 jails, including a juvenile detention center for the criminally insane—complete with little electrified, barbed wire fencing—and you have to pay $73.39 (exact change, please) when you pass, "GO…if you really want to…third door on the left." The winner is the first person to own a house, drink a bottle of corn liquor, and name all the passengers of the Titanic…in alphabetical order………Game with carrying case (plastic grocery bag)…$218.12

StrangeCo BUFFayola Crayons…..Not every product we market is manufactured by our employees. An explosion (StrangeCo was cleared of any involvement in this incident after five months of intensive questioning during a widely publicized Grand Jury Hearing on the matter) at the local crayon factory proved to be our windfall! A pack of 4703 pieces (some no bigger than a bread crumb) of plastic coated crayons, all black with little specks of metal in them. Comes in an attractive crumpled brown paper bag…like the kind bums carry booze in……………………………………………………………………$47.15

StrangeCo BUFFOONasketch…What do we come up with when we really don't care about what we are doing? Well, here ya go. A wonderful gift for the budding BUFFOON artist…. yeah right, as if. 43 paper grocery bags, haphazardly stapled together—voila!- a sketchpad! Comes with some sort of stick we found out back that marks the paper green, a small, irregular block of unrefined chalk and 17 or 18 partially charred charcoal briquettes…………………………………………………$36.11

StrangeCo BUFFOONabake Oven…. Sometimes just a small alteration, adjustment or modification to an existing product proves to be absolutely ingenious (and much better than the original, we say). Take this wonderful product. Instead of the measly wattage bulb that is normally used to bake those teeny cakes and pies, we use bulbs from abandoned lighthouses. 47,535 watts of power to make those cookies and cakes bake, burn and disintegrate in a matter of seconds…right before the cardboard and balsa wood oven severely overheats, explodes and burns down your home! Now THAT'S a toy!!....................$29.53

Just as I was about to turn the page to see more of these wonderful products especially designed for "Buffoons" (I was thinking of several people who definitely qualified as such), the phone rang. It took a couple of rings before I could find the portable phone (it was lodged between the refrigerator and the dishwasher) to answer it. It was my friend Gustav.

"Hey, Dash!! Did you get to watch TV today?! Man it was an incredible day! Right after Ultra Man—it was the one where his power stick, or whatever the hell that glowing cucumber thingy is called, shorts out and gives him too much power and Ultra Man turns into a semi-human, fur covered boy—Leave It To Beaver was on. Man that was so cool!! Beaver's dad gets thrown in jail because he was accused of organ harvesting! And that guy, Larry something…. Mondello, I think, ate a whole bushel of apples and spent the whole show sitting on the crapper!!"

I replied that I hadn't watched TV that day and that for the life of me, I couldn't recall doing anything at all that day except getting this really cool catalog. I asked him if he had seen it.

"Yeah! Isn't that so cool!? They just opened up one of their stores at the mall!! Man why don't we go over tonight? Let's go out to eat at that new Mexican place first. My cousin went there last week and he said it was really an experience. It was some girl's birthday, right? And you know how they always come to your table and sing and embarrass you? Yeah, well this place was better!! They have a group of midget waiters come up to you and put a sombrero on your head and then blindfold you! So, it's your birthday, right, you don't think too much of it, right? You think they're going to do something cool or funny or something, right? Well, these midget waiters start smacking this poor girl across her back with bamboo stalks! She starts crying like a teething child!! Then they started singing this song in Spanish, that my cousin said sounded like a cross between La Bamba and the Frito Bandito song from the commercial—you know the one, right? Yeah, man, let's go there then to that store. Whadda think?"

I told him that it sounded like a good idea but I didn't have any money.

"Well, Fuck you then!!"…and hung up the phone.

I awoke just then to the sounds of the neighbor mowing his lawn on his riding mower, singing "Lady" in his really bad Kenny Roger's voice through the police megaphone his wife got him for his birthday last month. Mickey, the neighbor, then points the megaphone at my window and still singing starts,

"Lazy…. You're my Lazy…Ass Neighbor…
Sleeping throughout the day
You may need an electric shock
Because you're so…
Lazy…You're My Lazy…Ass Neighbor"

He started laughing. I mean really laughing–the kind of laughter where you sometimes have a difficult time catching a breath and tears stream from your eyes. He laughed so hard he forgot to turn the wheel of the mower before he ran over and cut, shredded and multi-mulched his wife's prized gladiolas. She came running out of the house in a ratty looking flannel robe with cream all over her face, her hair in rollers and waving a plastic whiffle ball bat over her head. She was screaming as she final caught up to him and swatted him square in the back of the head so hard it bent the bat. My neighbor, with the megaphone still to his mouth yells out, "You crazy bitch!!" and jumps off the riding mower. He is face to face with his wife, both yelling at each other, as the mower continues through the yard, down the driveway and into the road where it is hit by a moving truck. I figured now would be a good time to go to the bathroom and take a shower as the driver of the truck jumped out of the cab carrying a wooden baseball bat. And I did.

* *

My favorite meat is lamb. I haven't found too many people outside my family who enjoy eating lamb. Something about eating "cute" animals. They, of course, have no problem eating a big, lazy, filthy beast, with germ-carrying flies swarming around it—like a cow; or a slovenly, foul smelling creature that eats rotten garbage and feces—like a pig. But a cute, innocent looking, little sheep—that seems much too nice to eat. And, well, you might as well say you worship the devil if you mention eating veal. Those poor, precious little calves stuffed into cramped, little boxes, crying out as they are in a constant state of panic —being near the point of suffocation from the intense heat and lack of fresh air, waiting to be slaughtered. Oh well. More for me.

When I planned a weekend visit to my girlfriend's, she said that she would cook lamb for me. She went through various cookbooks handed down from generation to generation, but there didn't seem to be any recipe for lamb. There were lots of other wonderful recipes though. Like one for Aunt Agnes and Louise's (though they both shared in the title, there was a terrible fight over who would be named first, injuring a family member and a farm animal before the riot squad showed up and arrested several people and shot the wounded creature) Miracle Bone Particle Muffins. There was also Cousin Corrine's Crushed and Creamed Cucumber Salad. The recipe for Uncle Bo Jack's Barbecued Gopher stuffed with Chicken Cartilage was about the closet thing to preparing lamb. She finally found an actual recipe specifically for lamb on the back of a newspaper clipping announcing a slightly tattered and torn shoe giveaway at the mall (my girlfriend loves shoes). Now she had to go find some lamb.

The local grocery chain didn't have lamb (even though sheep are raised for food a few miles down the road at a farm that had a big sign near the Interstate saying "American Lamb…Try It You'll Like It…For the Love of God, Please Eat Some!"), so she had the meat man with the snazzy white, blood stained (from a package of runny hot dogs that weren't properly manufactured) apron special order some lamb. 34 pounds of it. Being that it was being "special ordered", she had to wait a week to pick it up.

On the Wednesday before my arrival, she went back to the grocery store to pick up the product. It seems that Mr. Meatman made a slight error when ordering the meat and she was now stuck with double— 68lbs—the original amount of lamb. He was kind enough to only charge her for the original 34lbs. He was also kind enough to have the forklift bring the frozen mass of meat to her car. And he even helped her rip off the rubber seal around the trunk so that they could cram the lamb in using crowbars like one would use a shoehorn. He also helped her tie down her trunk with some string.

After managing to get the massive frozen "object" up to her third floor apartment (she utilized a make shift, block and tackle pulley system using 6 extension cords, a VCR tape box, and the caster wheels from the bottom of the lopsided television stand), she realized that she could not fit 68lbs of meat in her freezer. I don't know why she didn't realize that before she constructed the complicated lifting contraption out of household materials and managed to maneuver and haul up to the third floor an enormous and irregularly shaped frozen mass—with only some minor and superficial structural damage to the building—but nonetheless, she had to rid herself of approximately half the order of the most delicious meat God had ever placed on this great planet of ours. So she tossed it over the balcony railing into the woods. She told me after that weekend, there were roaming packs of rabid, wild dogs in her backyard for several days.

On my second day there, she perfectly prepared a small "hunk" of the meat (7 3/4 lbs) exactly the way I like it—rare—and I loved it! She on the other hand, fainted after seeing the blood and had to be brought around with a mega dose of potent smelling salts I always carry around for just such an occasion. After resting on the sofa with a cool towel on her forehead and her feet elevated for several minutes we continued eating, I having further cooked some of the lamb so that she could eat it. She actually liked it, which was good considering she would be eating lamb for the next 8 to 10 weeks! Later that evening the power went out.

Upon waking the next morning we were greeted to a freezer full of defrosted lamb and no air-conditioning. No air conditioning meant we had to open the windows to try to generate a breeze from the lovely 97-degree day outside. The only thing generated was a thick, heavy, powerful stench of rotting, baking in the sun, lamb carcass lying in the backyard. The only decision that seemed logical at the time was to try and cook all the meat in the gas stove and then freeze it for future use. So with damp rags over our noses and partially covering our eyes to keep them from watering as the nauseating fumes of dead lamb continued wafting in from the back, we stuffed the oven with a giant meat cube—which took up the entire inside of the oven—and cranked the temperature to 475 and got the hell out of the place. But, not before she passed out again and had to be brought around with the smelling salts.

We went to the $1.50 movie theater and bought tickets to see the documentary "TITANIC: Did it Really Sink? We Don't Think So" just so we could get inside from the oppressive Iowa heat. It felt so good in the air conditioning, that we both fell asleep as the film was just starting. We woke up six hours later when the ushers poked us (my girlfriend's snoring was annoying the other 5 moviegoers) with broom handles. The movie was still playing. We looked at the time and decided that we should go back and check on the lamb cube.

When we entered the apartment, we were happy to find that the power was back. The house smelled wonderful of the savory aroma of

the roasting blob of meat in the oven and the air conditioner was cooling the place—as well as the outdoors since we had forgotten to close
the sliding glass door before we left. Her balcony was covered with large
squirrels and colorful birds stretching and lounging, snacking on seeds
and nuts in the cool air emanating from the apartment. I slammed it
shut and all the animals outside just looked at me and—though I can't
be 100% sure—began crying.

We went into the kitchen and opened the oven door to see if this
wonderful smell was indeed coming from the lamb inside! It was! And
the meat—though greatly reduced in size as the fat had been cooked
out and had pooled in a big puddle in the front of the stove—looked
perfect! The true test would come in tasting it. We both grabbed a side
of the tub/pan and lifted it to the top of the stove. I grabbed a knife (the
one I found after looking in twelve drawers and six cabinets—including
the one over the top of the refrigerator that no one can ever reach) and
sliced off a perfectly cooked piece of roast lamb. Now, it wasn't as rare as
I typically enjoy my meat since we had to at least make an attempt to kill
any potentially life-threatening bacteria that may have thrived in the
meat, but was still very tender and juicy. I took a bite of the lamb and
was surprised to discover that it didn't taste bad. Didn't taste really good
either, but it was okay. It had some very faint after taste that I couldn't
figure out. But we decided to eat the damn thing anyway.

We sat down and ate lamb, 15 times cooked potatoes and green
beans. She drank wine straight out of the bottle (actually it was a box
with a faucet attached) while I drank vodka and Pepsi. We ate quite a bit
of the lamb and were feeling quite full. I went over to the sofa to lie
down for a minute while she cleaned the kitchen, a chore she is quite
accomplished in (you should see the way she is able to balance a broom
on her nose so she can clean the cobwebs in the corners of the ceiling).
I closed my eyes as she was saying something about having to finish eating the cake she had baked just for me. She began rattling off how the
cake was home made from the freshest and finest ingredients—and

actually started naming them. All of them. Each one. I believe I finally fell asleep when she got to the fully ripened and aged prune puree.... then I began to dream...

This particular dream had me in a very large shopping mall that I used to frequent quite often as a teen. We would spend untold hours walking around the mall following teen—age girls, sometimes as much as 27 miles an evening. We would sometimes actually manage to catch up to a couple and tried talking to them. There we were, grimaces on our faces from the pain streaking through our legs because our arches collapsed from all the walking, trying to be cool and talk the talk. We very rarely were successful. Once, one of the girls we actually managed to talk to, ran off to the pay phone to call for an ambulance, thinking that we may have been in an accident or were having seizures the way our faces contorted trying to mask the incredible pain. We would do it all again the next weekend, too.

In the dream, however, I am alone. I have in my hand a list of gifts to buy for individuals. I imagined that it must be Christmas time, but the mall had no decorations up—and believe me, they know how to do Christmas! One year, in addition to the 753,245 blinking lights they use to adorn the massive 63 foot tall "Hyperized Blue Spruce–Looking" artificial tree—which was made of T7 extruded aluminum (the kind they use on the space shuttle) and weighed 78 tons—and millions of ornaments ranging in size from the teeny plastic ice chip "stars" that fall gently from the ceiling to the massive 45 foot tall mechanical "Nut Cracker" which could crush a small diesel truck in it's massive, super— hydraulic jaws (show times—10 am and 4:45 pm, Mondays and Fridays), the mall installed a massive piece of machinery to actually make it snow inside.

The machine was designed by the defense department to create low-pressure systems in enclosed areas and cause specific weather conditions. The first day of operation at the mall was spectacular! It snowed actual snowflakes! People were walking around bundled in coats and gloves (it was a warm fall and early winter for us that year—about 72 degrees outside) laughing, making snowballs and slipping on their asses as highly polished and glazed terrazzo flooring and cold, wet ice make for extremely hazardous walking conditions. A few adventurous souls took some of the trays from the food court and proceeded to sled down the escalators. I believe that only 30 or 40 people were injured enough to be taken to hospitals. But the majorities of the people loved it and were making plans to bring whole families to the mall the next night.

The next night the mall was packed! I don't believe I have ever seen that many people in the mall before—not even the time when the brains at the mall scheduled to have the "Super Clearance" sidewalk sale and "Super Amnesty Day" (the day you could return anything you ever bought in the mall in the last 30 years and get a refund or exchange it for a brand new, similar item worth about 300 times what one originally paid for that piece of crap 8 track player with the attractive pseudo-wood panel casing bought 20 years ago) on the same day (they actually had to fly out the injured in helicopters as the parking lots and surrounding roads were jammed with vehicles). People were walking around, this time wearing more appropriate and properly tread footwear (and the mall did manage to spread some cinders around for better traction), and enjoying the winter wonderland in the mall. Couples holding hands and smiling, small children excited and laughing their laughter of youthful innocence.

Then something went horribly wrong.

It wasn't very noticeable at first—just some individuals' ears began "popping"—but you could feel something was changing. Something had malfunctioned in the weather machine causing a drastic drop of air pressure in the mall. The snow stopped and immediately turned to rain. A light drizzle at first, but within several minutes became a torrential downpour. People were scrambling to crowd into the stores slipping in slush and knocking each other over as the floor began flash flooding.

Then the pressure dropped further. You could hear a faint "pop" from the other end of the mall as one of the smaller shops' windows exploded. Then the sound became thunderous, as nearly all the stores' windows were shattering as the pressure inside the stores was greater than in the mall area. People began running out the doors to get out. They were streaming out of the mall as the pressure dropped even further. Some of those trying to escape were being sucked back in. The winds started kicking up as a tropical storm system formed in the center of the mall.

Seventy mile an hour winds began tossing the smaller individuals around like rag dolls along with millions of pieces of glass and Christmas ornamentation. The storm quickly developed into a category 5 hurricane with 159 mph sustained winds in the mall. Nearly everyone managed to get out of the mall as the hurricane moaned a deafening howl. The mall was nearly at the point of mass implosion when a maintenance worker tripped over the frayed extension cord the machine was hooked to and pulled out the plug. The storm stopped immediately. The people who came up with the idea were fired and the mall opened up again three months later.

In my dream, I begin looking at this list i have in my hand. I don't know exactly why I am buying so many gifts and the list looks unusual....

Aunt Marianna—a steel wool hat—(don't spend too much...remember last year she gave us a shiny new apple at Christmas)

Uncle Babbarosa—mechanical legs—(keeps dropping hints that his knees are hurting him a bit and wishes that he didn't have to use his legs anymore)

Grandma Poppachola—a mechanized bed that adjusts 50 different ways and can shoot people through the ceiling -(complains every day about how Grandpa Poppachola lays around in bed too long)

Grandpa Poppachola—a motorcycle helmet- (for when he gets shot through the ceiling)

Uncle Mussolini—one of those "lean cooking" frying contraptions—(keeps trying to reduce the fat in prosciutto by pressing it with a glowing red—hot cast iron frying pan, instead of, you know, just pulling it off like the rest of us do)

Cousin Giuseppe—a package of used, water soluble, temporary, cartoon character tattoos—(not even a thank you for the propane cannon we got him last year)

Cousin Olivia—a membership to the gym—(she said she wants to get down to 275lbs before the end of next year….yeah right!)

*********DON'T FORGET TO GET POPISICLE STICKS, PIPE CLEANERS, AND AQUARIUM ROCKS FOR AUNT WILIMINA'S ITALIAN EGG PASTRIES*********

The list didn't make much sense, especially since I don't even know whom these people were or why I am shopping for them. I kept walking through the mall and came to the center of the North Wing where there was a show going on to entertain the children and other shoppers who have lost their minds and wanted to see it. A big, pink rabbit with an ashy cigarette dangling from it's mouth area was just leaving the stage, waving to the children as the musical theme from the Winston cigarette ad ("Winston tastes good, like a cigarette should…") was playing extremely loud. Then a voice came over the sound system.

"Thank you, ladies and gentlemen, boys and girls. Razor Claws the Rabbit will be back in about 47 minutes! Wasn't that a great show!? Maybe we'll find out what he did with little Billy Adams when he comes back, huh, kids?"

The kids were clapping and stomping their feet and yelling at the top of their little lungs! Evidently, the over –sized, walking stuffed rabbit put on quite a performance. The kids were still screaming and yelling when the voice (I never saw who was at the microphone) came back over the speakers.

"Okay, now boys and girls, we have a very special person coming up next! He is a special, magical man and he will try to escape from certain death..right here!...in our special mall!! That is so cool! Shit yeah!! I can't wait! So without further ado, special ladies and gentle people, please put your hands together and help me extend a special, warm welcome to, The Amazing Jim Slippenshitz!!!"

The crowd was going crazy! Ladies were crying, kids were jumping up and down like wild kangaroos, men were cupping their hands to their mouths and yelling things like, "Yeah!! Jim!! You da man!!", "Come on, Babeeee!! Jimbo!! Show us what it's all about!!" "You da only one, Jim!! The ONLY ONE!! Yeah!!" and "You can do it, man!! You can DO it!! Whoop!! Hot Damn!!"

From behind the pretzel kiosk came Jim Slippenshitz. He looked to be about 55, short with a slumping posture, gray hair and was wearing some very thick-lensed glasses (he claimed they helped him look into the future as well as help him see well enough to recognize those dark figures in front of him as people). He had draped over his shoulders what looked to be a black shower curtain with the rings still attached. He walked up onto the stage and turned to face the audience, which was still in a state of hysteria. He lifted his arm to quiet the crowd and his "cape" fell open revealing that he was wearing yellow golf knickers and a Cheaptrick T-shirt underneath. He also had on black socks held up by garters (over the knickers) and white tennis shoes. He stepped up to the microphone in the center of the stage—actually the microphone bopped him in the head. He sounded like a pissed—off Ernest Borgnine.

"Is this thing on? Hello...hello...hello...Is this thing on? Testing...1...2...testing. Check...check...Hello? Hello? Will you shut the hell up so I can hear if this damn thing is on!? Why do you people have to be so damn ignorant? Jesus Christ, I'm getting too old for this shit!…I said shut you freakin' mouth…NOW!"

The crowd quieted down as they all looked towards the stage, mesmerized by this…figure. They all stared at him as if he were some sort of god or perhaps some sort of deranged evangelist. They all hushed to silence as Jim Slippenshitz lowered his hand and cleared his throat.

"All right, all right, shut up already. You people are becoming really annoying, you know that? I am getting tired of this shit. Alright, I'm gonna do the trick you probably all came here to see…The Amazing Escape From the Hermetically Sealed Plastic Cube Trick."

The crowd began going crazy again! Screaming and yelling!! One lady actually fainted. Whether it was from the mass hysteria of the crowd or because for a large woman she was wearing very small shoes, I'm not quite sure. The crowd then began chanting, "Cube Trick! Cube Trick!.." and clapping their hands in unison. Some of the adults looked dazed and glassy—eyed, holding up flaming lighters and swaying back and forth as if they were at a Grateful Dead concert or some sort of hash festival. There was a tremendous rush of humanity towards the stage when out from the Mary Jane's Mechanical Limbs and Smoked Ice Cream Emporium (I supposed that this was where I was to purchase the mechanical legs for Uncle Babbarosa—whoever the hell he was. I did hear someone mention that they have a real killer nacho and barbecue flavored milk shake.), three mall maintenance workers rolled out a large red plastic cube.

"Over here will be fine," began directing Jim Slippenshitz speaking directly into the microphone that could be heard through out that sector of the mall and the food courts of the 3 out of the 7 remaining mall sectors. "No…Over here…Yes you, jackass, over here. No…. what are you doing? Do you understand the English?…Over-a Here-io…What are you, a mental deficient?"

The crowd began laughing, and I assumed they were thinking it was part of the show, but the magician seemed genuinely perturbed. The three maintenance workers were acting like they were being put out by actually having to perform some work. A woman next to me, carrying a very large buffalo wing flavored ice cream waffle cone in one hand and a computer generated picture of her face superimposed onto Farah Fawcett's body on a calendar in the other, was telling me that the lead janitor, Homer, was voted the "Laziest Human Being to Ever Hold A Job and Temporarily At Least, Remain Off Welfare," by his fellow maintenance workers at the local Janitors, Security Guards, Road Repair Crews and Others Who Get Paid for Being Idle union meeting last month.

She was telling me that he so hated the labor involved in replacing paper products in the restroom dispensers, that he would stand at the bathroom doors while people were using the facilities to make sure they would only use only 3 squares of one ply toilet tissue and one paper towel per visit. He also encouraged the restroom patrons to flap their arms like a huge bird and let the air dry their drenched hands. He was forced to stop that, however, after one person dislocated her shoulder while flapping her hands with extreme vigor in a vain attempt to create a breeze strong enough to dry her face.

The three of them managed to maneuver the plastic cube to where Jim Slippenshitz, after some harsh words and aggressive and obscene hand and arm gestures, had wanted the figure moved. The three of them just slumped to the floor in states of exhaustion, acting as if they had just moved a loaded cement truck with flat tires up a mountain rather than an 18 lb, colored piece of plastic, on wheels, across 25 feet of level, polished mall floor.

"Well, thank you, gentlemen. You bunch of lazy ass bastards! Look at ya! Aren't you ashamed to be alive?! Good lord, I've never seen a bunch of sorrier people in my life. Hey, you…yeah you…Homer, right? Yeah, I though so. Ladies and Gentlemen, behold the laziest creature in the universe, Homer the Jackass! The man who wants to find an easier way to breathe so he doesn't have to move his chest muscles so much! Stand up and take a bow, you sack of shit, or are you too fuckin' lazy to do that! God, you guys make me want to vomit!! Disgusting!! Simply Vile!! Horrible creatures! A waste of blood and bones!! Okay, now remember you guys, I'm going to need your help in couple of minutes with this complicated trick…see if you can stay awake for the next 45 to 90 seconds!"

Just as the three lazy maintenance workers managed to struggle to get the lid off the plastic cube, the lady standing next to me dropped her huge waffle cone on my foot. She immediately bent down and tried to rescue the cone, using the photo calendar to pick up the melting blob of buffalo wing flavored chocolate ice cream with vanilla sprinkles and chopped fennel seeds. I told her not to worry about it as she began smearing the ice cream into my shoes as she tried to wipe them clean. My socks were getting wet and sticky and I was getting embarrassed—for me and for this pathetic woman trying to eat her cone and wipe up my shoes and the mall floor with her crappy novelty gift.

I left the crowd and walked over to a kiosk that sold packaged, processed and preserved smoked meat logs and assorted cheeses and asked the teen age girl behind the chuck wagon wheel if she had a napkin that I could use. She said that they don't allow people who don't buy any smoked meats or cheeses to have use of the paper products. She informed me that the special of the week was a Bahamian Cart Mule liver and smoked blood sausage and asked me if I would like to try a free sample. I declined and said that I need to get to the restroom to get the crap off my shoes. She told me that there would probably not be enough paper towels in there for the mess I had. She was kind enough, however to reach into her pocketbook and hand me a moist and tattered Kleenex. I thanked her and turned to go to find something to clean up.

As I turned, I saw that there was a commotion going on at the other end of the sector. I forgot about the ice cream on my shoes and headed to see what noise was about. I managed to get through the crowd and saw some sort of trough, about 30ft long and 3ft wide, filled with smoldering red coals. I couldn't get too much closer as the heat was singeing my eyebrows and the hair in my nose. I took a few steps back as my eyes were drying rapidly, causing me to blink uncontrollably. After a few seconds away from the intense heat and dusting away from my forehead the remains of my eyebrows, my eyes re-hydrated and I could see what was going on.

There was an Indian (from the country of India, not like an Indian who runs a casino, wears feathers on his head and smokes 'em peace pipe) gentleman wearing what looked to be a big diaper wrapped around his torso and a white hotel towel ("Property of the Des Moines Hotel and Big Farm Equipment Tire Outlet" was written on the towel in what looked like black laundry marker) on his head, turban style. He climbed up the one step to the beginning of the trough and turned to the audience.

"Watch dis," he says in a heavy Brooklyn accent, "I am now goin' to show all youse dat da mind has power over da body. If any of youse has, like, heart conditions, you should, like…go away…or say like any of youse pregnant chicks might wanna turn ya heads….so youse, you know, don't puke on my show. Okay…beware da mysteries of da mind!"

He turns to face the length of the trough, holds his arms out to the sides and closes his eyes. He stood there for a few seconds and then took a deep breath. He lifted one foot over the hot coals and slowly placed it down. He then began walking briskly over the coals. At about the 15 ft mark he opened his eyes and smiled to the audience. He waves as he continues walking. "Look!! I'm doin' it! I'ze actually walkin' on da friggin' coals here!"

At the 20ft mark he grabs his left calf and screams, "Crap! I gotta friggin' charley horse!!" as he stands on one foot on the 1500 degree bed of coals. He begins hopping on the foot screaming unintelligible obscenities as the smell of burning flesh begins to emanate from his sizzling and smoking right foot. He managed to get to the side of the trough and simply fell to the ground to escape the extreme heat from the trough that was under him. The crowd began to "boo" loudly as he was writhing in agony on the mall floor. "What a crock of shit!" said the guy next to me. "What kind of message does that send to our kids?!" I told him I didn't know what the hell he was talking about and didn't he think that maybe someone should help the guy on the floor with the charred foot howling like an injured moose.

Just then, the Indian from Brooklyn stood up and turned to face the crowd. He is smiling and doesn't seem to be in any pain. The crowd is silenced in awe. "What the fuck is this?!" says the guy next to me. The crowd all looked at him and gave him a collective "Sssshhh!!". Everyone just looked at the Indian, still smiling and turning side to side slightly so all the crowd in front of him could see his smile. He then steps to one side and keeps only his right arm up. He looks to the crowd and says, in perfect, un-Brooklynese English. "Ladies and Gentlemen. You stand there and look at me in awe! You're amazed and baffled! Your mind is racing in disbelief! Well, prepare to be truly amazed!! Ladies and gentlemen…Jim Slippenshitz!!"

From the middle of the trough full of glowing red hot coals popped up Jim Slippenshitz the magician! The crowd is in hysteria!! People screaming as if they have just lost their minds! Men and women simply began collapsing to the floor in shock as Jim Slippenshitz jumped down from the scorching trough and dusted ashes and smoldering embers from his partially melted and shrunken shower curtain/cape. The crowd began screaming louder…howling the moans of the damned. This was getting a little scary. Some began pulling their hair out in clumps. Suddenly, they all headed to the exits and ran into the night screaming…except me. I stood there in front of Jim Slippenshitz and the Indian from Brooklyn wearing the diaper like an infant and the hotel towel on his head. The Indian was still smiling straight ahead. He wasn't looking at anyone, just staring straight ahead. I looked at him for a few seconds. I turned my head and there was Jim Slippenshitz right in front of me!

I quickly turned away and began to run from him towards the other end of the mall. I saw the stage where Jim Slippenshitz was supposed to have been performing his trick. I saw the big, plastic cube sitting up on the stage and it's rocking back and forth. From inside I heard "Hey can somebody get us out?! Help, we're stuck in here!! The magic guy's assistants!! You gotta help us!!"

I approached the box and simply lifted the lid, which must have weighed all of 2 ½ pounds, and saw the three maintenance workers all crammed together inside. I asked them why didn't they simply lift the lid and get out. "Cause we're too fucking lazy, man! And we're on our break!! We can't be lifting stuff like that when we are on break!! Union rules!" replied Homer. I turned again to run and there was Jim Slippenshitz with a big Arabian saber sword in his hand.

The next thing I know, I am on my girlfriend's sofa and the TV is on. That is odd because my girlfriend didn't have cable and hence, had no broadcast television (except for a fuzzy channel that only broadcasts the spot prices for hog bellies and such). But she did have a VCR, so I assumed that she had put in a tape. In the kitchen I hear my girlfriend still rattling off ingredients to the cake.

"And Aunt Behalia's big secret to the subtle taste is the perfect blend of Tab, bleach, and those big tablets of chlorine used in routine pool maintenance," I heard her say. As I tried to determine what was going on, it dawned on me that I was still dreaming. I was feeling very confused, wondering what had happened to the magician and the mall. I then glanced at the TV and saw that a Winnie the Pooh cartoon was playing. I grabbed the remote which was right there in front of me on the coffee table (now I know I was dreaming) and turned up the volume on the television.

Pooh was slumped up against an old oak tree with his eyelids drooping considerably as if he were suffering the wrath of a hangover. Owl was on the branch above and slightly off to the side of his head so the bear didn't have to move to see him. There were leaves blowing around and an infamous "Pooh Honey pot" laying on its side, evidently empty.

"Well, Pooh, it appears that you have indulged yourself again with another visit to the 100 Acre Woods bordello last night," said Owl in a somewhat condescending tone of voice.

"Well…it would appear that you are correct…again, Owl," replied Pooh with a rather drawn out tempo. "It seems that I am not able to shake this…thing I have for the loose women. I believe it is all a result of this absurd insulin and glucose imbalance that I have. I think that it is because all I ever eat is honey. I could certainly use some right now."

"Pooh, you certainly must understand what you are doing is of very low ethics, not to mention somewhat dangerous."

"Yes, I believe you are right…again, Owl. How is it that you know everything? Perhaps if I had completed my education past the first grade, didn't consume alcohol so much, shied away from the marijuana, put an end to inhaling aerosol fumes, and could—how should I put it–'keep it in my pants' for more than 10 minutes at a time, I would know more. Don't you think that to be true, dear Owl? Oh bother…I believe that that one hoochie I was with last night, Shaniqa, I believe her name was—no, it was Rosalita —now there is some very sweet honey—absconded with my billfold and credit cards."

"You are a sad, pitiful, little bear, Pooh," said Owl as he flew off the branch.

"Yes…and you are—how do i say this?- a pile of camel crap that has sprouted wings, Mr. Owl," sighed Pooh as Piglet came running towards him with a panicked look upon his puny face and large beads of perspiration flying off his brow.

"P-p-p-p-p-p-ooh! Oh, geez! P-p-p-p-p-ooh!" stammered the picayune walking ham, Piglet. "P-p-p-p-p-oooh!! You have to, you have to, you have to run!!! Oh, Christopher R-r-r-r-ob-b-b-in has lost his, his, his mind!!"

"Piglet," started Pooh, barely moving, "may I ask that the next time you come to see me, you would be so kind to bring along an interpreter, since I have very little to no idea what you ever say? Perhaps if you were to loosen that annoying scarf, you would be able to speak somewhat clearer. Oh, and by the way, did you ever notice, my dear Piglet, that your ears are bigger than your head? Tell me, is that a normal occurrence for a filthy beast such as yourself?"

"But, P-p-p-p-ooh," continued Piglet, seemingly taking no offense to the insults laid upon him by the hung over Pooh bear, "Christopher R-r-r-r-o-b-b-in wants to, to, to kill y-y—ou!!"

"Oh, Poppycock and hogsquash, my dear Piglet," replies Pooh, barely able to keep his drooping eyes open, "Everyone knows that Christopher Robin is a very dear friend of mine. And, my giant eared little friend, you are also aware that he tends to—how do i say this?–'lose control' a bit whenever he misses his hourly infusion of Ritalin. This certainly must be one of those very infrequent occasions."

"Oh, no, Pooh," chimed in the little kangaroo, Roo, who appeared out of nowhere and startled Pooh, now sitting upright, "Piglet is right!! Christopher Robin says he is going to—let me see how did he say it?...."

"He said he's going to kill you and chop your fat, matted—fur carcass into a million pieces," moaned (in his notoriously annoying monotone, bass voice), Eeyore (the sluggish, sloth of a beast who would be paid a complement if he were to be called a 'good–for–nothing lazy jackass'), "I heard the whole thing, Pooh. He's surely going to kill you. Sorry to see you go."

"First of all, Roo, please don't up and scare me like that. I nearly soiled myself. And Eeyore, my incredibly morose acquaintance, I am sure that you heard something, but is it possible that you have misunderstood?" asked Pooh, now a little bit more alert (his eyes are wide open from the start he got from Roo).

"Oh no, Pooh, he understood perfectly," said Kanga (who also appeared out of nowhere), in an oh so pleasant tone of voice, "I'm afraid, what everyone has been telling you is correct, Pooh. Christopher Robin most decidedly intends to kill you. And I believe that he is on his way here now."

"Oh, Mommy, Mommy, can I stay and watch Christopher Robin chop Pooh up?" the little Roo asked Kanga, "I wanna take a piece of him into show and tell tomorrow!!"

"Roo!! What has become of you?!!" shrieked Kanga, in her mother like voice, "Haven't you had enough violence? Wasn't it enough that you were there when Pooh killed Rabbit last winter? You saw the gaping shotgun holes in that poor creature. Why must you see more?!?"

"Now, Kanga, you all know that was an accident. I had no intention of actually killing Rabbit. I merely intended to scare him into giving me some more honey. I was in a terrible frame of mind, don't you recall? I hadn't had honey in two days and I was suffering terrible from detoxification. I simply had to have more honey!!" said Pooh, a bit upset that someone would bring up such an unfortunate moment in the history of The 100 Acre Wood. He was now standing, swaying a bit, and trying ever so hard to maintain his balance. "I would never imagine that the gun had ammunition in. I assure you now, as I have on countless occasions in the past, that it was a most unfortunate incident, nothing more."

"Yeah, whatever you say, Pooh. I hope you rot in hell," said the sweet Kanga.

From over the hill in the distance one could see a figure bouncing around in no apparent direct direction, but was coming closer to Pooh and the others. In the background cartoon music was playing and the "boing" sound used to indicate a spring being sprung. Or the arrival of Tigger. He was now very close and I heard the "boing" sound a lot louder and Tigger uttering a string of "WooHoos" and wheezy giggles. He came running into Pooh, bowling him over and sitting right on top of the bear.

"Helloooo, Poo -poo-a-roo, my bosom bestus buddy, old friend…woohoo!! Looking a bit under the weather there, Pooh boy.

Woohoo!! A little bit too much honey, hey there, Poohbaloo?! Eeck!! I hate that stuff!! That stuff will kill you, ya know? I heard that there was a bear outside the 100-Acre Wood place that just exploded...BOOM...(throwing his hands up in the air and falling backwards off of Pooh)...woohoo...well, you get the picture, I'm sure."

"Tigger, my friend, why must you knock me over every time you come to see me? Oh bother, I think that you may have caused me to rupture a disc," said the prone Pooh, "Could you...would you.... please, Tigger, lend me some assistance to get up?"

Tigger bounced over and helped Pooh stand up, using his hands on top of his flailing arms to dust the bear off.

"Sorry about there, Poohbobochuck! There!! Woohoo, now you don't look so bad...woohoo...for a bear that's all hopped up on...woohoo...demon honey that is!! Woohoo, I crax myself some-times, ya know? Now what did I come up here for?...Hmmmm, what could it be? Hmmmm.... Oh yeah!! Nows I remember!! Christopher Robin was running this way, right behind me as a matter of fact, carry-ing an ax!! He was trying to kill me, I think!! But my keen Tigger skills helped me to elude the men -ee- ma -neye-a -calicle...woohoo...boy killer!!"

"But Tigger," piped in Roo, "Christopher Robin doesn't want to kill you!! He wants to kill Pooh!!"

"Oh, he does, does he? Well, we'll see ab...wait a minute, there little spring boy...did you say he wasn't going to kill me?" asked Tigger raising his right eyebrow really high and leaning towards the baby kangaroo.

"That's right, he doesn't want to kill you, Tigger," replied Roo, "You're just a big goof. Nobody wants to kill you. Well, Rabbit did, but he's (looks over to Pooh) dead now.... isn't he, Pooh?"

"Phew!! Woohoo!! Ah life is so sweet!! Sorry about you there, Poohpapala, but we, you know, all have to go sometimes. Woohoo!! And Rabbit was a pain in the ass, anyways. Always worried about his rotting cabbages and ridipidiculous carrots and.... stuff. Good riddance I say!!

So good ole Chris is going to kill you, huh, Pooh? That's a crying shame. But…woohoo, watcha gonna do?"

"He'll probably miss you and get me instead, woe is me," moaned the gloomy ass, Eeyore, "I can feel death for me is very near."

"Well, Eeyore," said Pooh, his voice raising in irritation as his eyes begin to glower (I remember thinking how cool it was to see Pooh getting ticked), "If Christopher Robin comes here and doesn't kill anyone, I will make it a point to kill you myself!"

"Murderer!!" shouts Kanga as she grabs Roo and starts hopping away with her offspring bouncing on the ground, his face contorting in obvious pain he was receiving from the punishing beating his body was taking— being slammed repeatedly on the ground and his arm being pulled from it's socket.

"Bitch!!," screams Pooh.

"P-p-p-p-oooh…my b-b-b-uddy (sob), I'mmmm gonna r-r-really m-m-m-iss you," moaned the freak of a pig, openly weeping.

"What, Piglet?!" snapped a perturbed Pooh, "I don't understand…A…. SINGLE….. WORD….. YOU….. SAY!! Good Lord, please, take some speech therapy!! But for now, KEEP YOUR MOUTH SHUT!"

"Woohoo!! Well, time for me to go b-b-b-bouncing around!! Cause that's what we Tiggers do best!!…Woohoo.."

Music started swelling in the background and Tigger began to sing…

"Ohhhh…the wonderful thing about Tiggers,
Is Tiggers are a wonderful beast,
Their eyes are made of croutons
Their brains are made out of yeast
Their blood is full mustard
Their kidneys are full of bleach
Their toes are always crooked
They all have terrible speech

But the most wonderful, wonderful, wonderful thing about Tiggers,
Is that I'm the only...."

At the exact moment he went to utter the word "one", an ax came
down upon him from behind with such force that it split Tigger in half.
Piglet let out a blood curdling scream and grabbed his humongous ears,
pulling them down over his eyes—and over his nose, mouth, chin and a
good portion of his scrawny little neck—they were indeed very big ears.

"Well, it's about time you got here," muttered Eeyore, "Hurry up and
kill him already, then you can kill me, too."

"Oh, why don't you just shut your goddamn mouth, you ass!" shouts
Christopher Robin his hair all tussled, raising the ax with little bits of
Tigger stuck on it over his left shoulder, "Now get the fuck out of here or
I will kill you!! Go!!! (Sniff)...What the hell is that smell? Piglet?...Did
you shit your pants? Again? What the hell is wrong with you? What are
you an animal? HA HA.. I guess you are!!

"Well, Pooh bear! You know that I have to kill you, don't you?" continued Chris Robbin,

"Your outrageous behavior is atrocious!! Screwing at the whore-
house, smoking all the plants...KILLING for God's sake!! Oh yeah, you
definitely have to go!! Just like your ole pal Tigger here!!"

"Listen here, you insolent, hyperactive, attention deficit disorder little bastard," snorted Pooh as he got into what could be described as a
martial arts pose—though an awfully bad one, "You aren't going to do
anything and you know it!!"

"Oh yeah? Well, here we go, fattalina tubalardo!!" yells Chris Robbin
as he charges towards Pooh, ax raised over his head.

Just then there was a knock on the door and I immediately got up to
open it. There was some guy carrying a black sample case in his left
hand and a sample of something in a white plastic container (like a cold
cream jar). Good lord, I though, a salesman. He just looked straight at
me and began spewing out words in a steady, monotone voice...

"Thank you sir for opening your door. You have such a lovely home. It is obvious that you are a meticulous house cleaner, miss. (There was only me at the door) Wouldn't you like to have in your home, the same cleaner that they used to clean up the slight mishap at Chernobyl? I am sure that you to. This amazing product (He is now holding the product in front of my eyes) has the cleaning capability of the sun. It is safer than Plutonium and a smidge less volatile than nitroglycerin. It will clean any stain that you may have in your home. It can clean barnacles off the hulls of steamships. It can remove varicose veins and unsightly blemishes. It just plain eats mold right off your bathroom floor. It can be used to remove bugs, tar and even the cars original paint right down to the bare metal. There is nothing this wonderful product can't clean. Allow me to demonstrate."

He walks right past me into the living room. My girlfriend is still rattling of the ingredients to her "magical" cake as the salesman reaches into his sample case and pulls out a jar of dark liquid and removes the lid. The smell makes my eyes water. He continued in his monotonous drone.

"This, madam and or sir, is a solution we created at our laboratories. It is a combination of ingredients that will cause a stain that will never be removed. It contains used car oil, machine lubricants, mashed blueberries, grape juice, coffee grounds and several industrial, indelible, toxic dyes. Our cleaner will get rid of all the stains this vile potion will cause."

He then begins splashing the fluid all over the apartment. A big stain on the sofa, dark liquid streaming down the walls, a large, wet stain on the carpet. And the smell was horrible! He puts the empty jar back in his sample case and turns to me with the product in his hand.

"Sorry about this, but I have brought the wrong product. I forgot that I no longer sell the cleaning potion. I got fired two weeks ago. I now sell this amazing instant tooth filling concoction. Would you like to buy some?"

As I turned my head to look at the mess again (a slightly dense fog was beginning to develop from the fluid), he dropped his sample case and dental filling stuff and ran out the door and down the stairs to his car. I could hear the squealing of tires as I headed out the door to get to the stairs, realizing that I would never get him. I came back into the apartment and looked at the smelly mess all over the place. My girlfriend had just finished with her ingredients…

"…and a whole tube of that water based lubricating jelly. I think that's everything."

I turned back to the TV and saw The 100 Acre wood on fire. Flames were shooting up into the air, animals running out in panic, their fur smoldering. Thunderous "booms" could be heard as trees were exploding when the internal sap boiled and escaped from the intense heat. Helicopters were dropping those huge shovel- buckets of water, but they were barely putting a dent in the inferno. Good lord, I thought to myself, this is horrendous!!

I wake up to my girlfriend pinching me, yelling, "You better not even be sleeping!! I have 20lbs of cake sitting here, and you're gonna eat it all before you go back, you hear?"

I spent the remainder of my stay eating lamb and cake until I nearly ripped the lining of my intestinal cavity.

SECTION III

So, Uh, Now What?

"Okay, so you spent how long on this amazing project of yours?" asked my best friend.

"I guess pretty close to 20 years," I replied, knowing that he was setting me up for some sort of slam.

"I see...20 years, huh? And this is it?"

"Well, I mean, I have a whole bunch of other dreams, but most are either way too short, or extremely lacking in detail. After all, the whole point was to see what foods would create those incredibly vivid dreams," I managed to spout out as I started to feel my face get flush and a slight sweat break out.

"And did you figure out what foods caused specific dreams?"

"Uh, no, not really," I muttered as the sweat started beading on my forehead, "the most vivid dreams occurred whenever I mixed contrasting foods, period. Mostly high in sodium and preservatives. And, oh yeah, eating a lot of it!"

"So, if I understand this, and please, Dash, correct me if I am wrong...you spent—what was it? 20 years, right?—20 years eating a bunch of crazy–ass foods then going to sleep then you would write it down in a cheesy spiral notebook?"

"Well, yeah, except, you know, I moved on from the notebook a long time back. It's all on computer disk now!"

"Okay, so now it's on a computer disk. Well, there you go then! Now it must be research!" Spewed my friend with false exuberance and sarcasm so freakin' thick his words seemed to drip off him and puddle on the floor.

"Now, I'm sure that my studies don't come close to finding a cure for viral hemorrhagic fever, or, let's say, discovering a method that would keep preserved animal matter in a suspended and liquefied state so some 'scientist' can add his magical 'soda gas' to it and put it in a can so the world can enjoy a highly unique taste treat!" I shot back with my salvo of sarcasm, but not even close to what my friend can dole out.

"Are you mocking me and my highly regarded studies in the field of Dairy Carbonation?" he asked with a distinctly serious look on his face.

"Yeah, I am. Highly regarded, my ass!" I replied.

"Uh, huh, I see, " he mumbled as he hung his head, eyes at the floor, " let's all make fun of the guy who finished college, went on to graduate school and has done some honest–to–God research!" I thought he was going to cry.

"Awww…Boo hoo fuckin' hoo! Go cry somewhere else! I did research. I know it, end of story!"

"Is it?" he asked, no longer with the cry baby face on and looking up from the floor.

"What are you talking about?" I asked, quite curious as to where he was going to go now.

"Well, you said you just completed a shit load of research, right?"

"Yeah…. so?" Waiting for him to get to the slam.

"So, uh, now what?" he queried in that annoying whine and silly smirk on his face.

Hmmmm…. Good question. Now what? It wasn't something I had taken the time to really think about. Sure, there were times I envisioned myself speaking at a symposium somewhere about my magnificent discoveries, but I really never actually thought of it becoming a reality! Maybe I should show it to someone. Someone who might be able to pass it on to a scientific club, or group, or whatever they call a organization of eggheads.

"You might want to take it to a publisher," offered my friend.

"You think someone would want to publish this?" I asked, realizing too late that he suckered me in.

"Fuck no!" he snorted. Hit that nerve again. I don't know why he does that to himself. My friend had been trying for years to get something published. Nothing. He did manage to get a mention in the 'Someplace Or Other Science Journal' when his picture appeared along with a short article on how he had to be dragged out of a Regional Conference on Synthetic Caramel Flavorings since he refused to stop talking about a recent "breakthrough" he had in the development of large mouth trout fungicides. The article mentioned that no one cared since (and even I knew this) large mouth trout didn't suffer and fungal problems.

"Why would someone want to publish that crap you came up with?" continued my friend.

"I don't know. But I think I'll try to find out."

My friend made it perfectly clear by ranting and screaming and using some crazy arm gestures (in some extremely quick motions that developed enough static electricity to make his normally flaccid hair virtually straight up) that he was not going to give me the names of the "serious" scientific publishers he had approached in the past—even though I hadn't asked and the thought of doing so never entered my mind. I could find publishers on my own! So, I broke out the Yellow Pages and began looking....

Well, that didn't help much. There weren't many publishers to speak of. They listed some that published little rags, cheap news leaflets and such, but no real publishers. It didn't occur to me to look on the Internet to see if I could find anything until I was about to toss that freakin' useless bunch of paper out the freakin' window. I sat down at my computer, made sure it had enough diesel fuel (that's just an inside joke in reference to the amazingly slow speed my system runs—it actually runs on a turbine that I pedal under the keyboard) and started looking. Then I found about thirty thousand or so publishers. I narrowed it down to scientific publishers. 9,257 results. Crap. I thought that I might want to actually go to the publisher with my material, therefore I narrowed the search down to the Philadelphia vicinity. 57. I wanted closer. Within 30 miles of my home in Bryn Mawr. Three. That's better.

One publisher was listed as being right down the street from me in Ardmore, Pennsylvania. That would be real convenient! I called and got that pleasant recording from the phone company telling me that this number was no longer in service and that there was no forwarding number. They probably went out of business publishing crap like my friends theories on carbonated cheeses and such, I chuckled to myself. On to number Two. The guy who answered that line seemed inebriated. I asked if this was "Sci-Guys Publishing."

"Didja shay, gay guys polishing?" slurred the sot on the other end.

"No. SCI-Guys Publishing. Publishing. Like books, ya know?" I continued, realizing that this was definitely not the place I was looking for.

"Nice guys blushin'? NO, I don' see no nice guys blushin' here. Hold a sec and I'll see if there's any nice guys polishing, or blushin' or whatever…hold on…," he held the phone away from his face and yelled out into what apparently was a bar, "HEY! HEY! Lishen, there's a gay guy on the phone and I thing he wants a polishin'…any nice guys in here?"

In the background, all one can hear is the bellowing and screams of those who have consumed a touch too much of the alcohol. "Tell, him to go fuck himself" and "Hey old man, you getting yourself a date?" were a couple that came through clearly amidst the laughter and shouting. I was tempted to wait for the old man to address me again on the phone just for the hell of it, but I did have one more lead I had to follow up on: Serious Body of Knowledge Press located in Norristown, Pennsylvania. Near the library where I started this magnificent journey!

I called the number and a rough, feminine voice answered. It sounded more like a man pretending in a slight falsetto voice to be a woman. "Serious Body of Knowledge Press and Mind Expansion University, how may I help you?"

"Uh, yes, I have some scientific research that I have recently completed and I would like to speak to someone about having my work published."

"Oh, how nice for you. You must be very proud! Well, are you in the area?" she/he asked.

"Why, yes, I am only a few miles away. Would I be able to come in today?"

"Well, let me check Dr. Balzich's schedule to see if he has time available today. He is a very busy man. Always working on something of great importance to humankind! Hmmmm....looks like he has some time free at 2:30. Would that be acceptable?"

"Yes, yes of course, that would be fine!" I replied a bit surprised that I would be able to see someone so soon. I would have just enough time to have my material printed out and get across town to meet with Dr. Balzich. It then occurred to me how funny that name was. (Balzich? Why, yes they do. Do you mind terribly if I scratch them?) Almost burst into laughter on the phone.

"Well, then, let's make it an official appointment," she continued. I should talk to this Balzich guy about this lady he has answering his phone. It dawned on me that I would probably be seeing this, this....woman...man...whatever when I went to see the guy. Could prove to be a most interesting day. Oh yeah, it would be something all right.

"May I have your name, sir?" the receptionist asked.

"Yes, of course, that would help, wouldn't it? It's Gabelli. Dashel Gabelli. One "B", two "Ls" (Although my name is spelled exactly like it sounds, since I was a child, everyone has asked me to spell it). You said 2:30, correct?" Nothing on the other end for what seemed an eternity (but was actually only like 10—15 seconds). "Hello? You still there?" I asked.

"Oh, yes, yes...sorry for that delay. I, uh dropped my pen or some-thing...yes, yes, Mr.....Gabelli, is it? Yes, of course it is. 2:30 is correct. We'll see you then. Bye." And she abruptly hung up the line. And she...he...whatever...sounded a little funny there before the call was terminated. A little bit more of a crackly, masculine voice. I pushed that thought to the back of the old mind as I hurried to find the disk and get it printed out.

I arrived at the place at 2:25. I usually like to show up early, but not too early that it appears that I have nothing else to do (which was the case that particular day anyway) and found only one vehicle (one of those teeny Renaults that was all the rave in Europe—where gas is like $75 a gallon—but they stopped shipping them here in the mid 70's cause they kept getting stuck under the axles of hooptys—the big Lincolns and Mercurys that clogged the highways during the time that gas was plentiful and giant vehicles were the norm) in the small parking area located behind the old building. I parked my car (a red SAAB 900s, if you really care to know) next to the teeny metal box with wheels, gathered my papers and headed around to the front of the building to the entrance.

The front of the building faced Main Street in Norristown and in the short walk from coming around the corner of the building to the entrance—maybe 50—60 feet—I came across a wino slumped up against the building, a filthy young man with long, straggly hair that went down to his waist playing a xylophone with two screwdrivers, and a hooker that was wearing those really classy fishnet stockings that have numerous holes in them and stiletto heeled shoes that look like they've seen better days. I stepped over the sleeping bum clutching his brown bag of liquid dreams, threw a couple of quarters into the hat that the dirty xylophone player had laying on the side walk and averted my eyes away from the hooker who smiled at me with yellowing, crooked and gapped teeth and was about to ask me if I wanted a good time or what ever vernacular whores use to make sure you know that they are there to make you happy. Or sick. A toss up, really. I saw the door with the words "Serious Body of Kno edg Pre and Mind Expan on Un ersity" and underneath that jumble of letters was "Editor n hief: Franklin P. Balzich, Ph.D."

From outside, the front of the building looked like an old department store that lined old city streets. A full glass front so you can observe whatever it is they wish to push onto the public (usually some piece of clothing manufactured with the very best synthetic fabrics available to man stretched over some mannequin that has a chipped nose and color fading from its painted plaster head and only two and half fingers on the only hand), but in this case, the windows were blocked out with black film (the kind we use down south to keep the internal temperatures of our automobiles from reaching the "flash point" where the upholstery would self combust) that was seriously bubbling, but prevented one from seeing any of the goings on inside.

The door, with the missing letters, was also a film-covered glass door. As I opened it, I was hit with a strong musty smell and it took a few seconds to adjust to the lack of lighting in the building. The reception desk was there, off to the right, but there was no sign of the she/male that had answered the phone when I had called earlier. I took quite a few steps beyond the desk into the semi darkness of a hallway when he appeared.

He stepped out from a door (that looked an awful like a cheap closet door with a dinky knob on it that they don't even install in rat trap apartments you would find in ghettos) off to the left and took a few steps into the lighter part of the room. Then he just stood there for a few moments, not saying anything. I looked at him trying to figure out whether I should say anything, approach him, or what. He looked to be about 50 or so, with a receding hairline, but otherwise dark hair (probably dyes it, I thought—as if I should talk—dying my hair blonde to keep the gray at bay. Hey! It works, right? I mean I don't look like an idiot, do

I? Never mind, don't answer.). He was wearing a white lab coat and dark framed glasses and for a moment looked like Jerry Lewis when he played that professor—I don't remember the name of the movie or character off hand. And for another moment, he looked awfully familiar.

"Mr. Gabelli, I presume?" he asked. Good Lord, that voice sounded real familiar! I tried to place it, and after a few seconds it occurred to me that it sounded a lot like the receptionist's!

"Yes, yes it is. Dr. Balzich? I'm sorry, I thought that your receptionist would be here (trying to nail him on this). I wouldn't have come towards your work area otherwise. She had told me how exceptionally busy your are."

"Ah, yes, Marlene had to take off to tend to her child who had ingested the bottom part of the chair leg, you know the part that helps the chair slide on the floor, during recess at school," he stated as if trying to develop a story as he went along, "Quite a odd child actually. The child will eat virtually anything. Why, only last week Marlene was called away again when the school called stating that her precious young one had eaten nearly half of an industrial filter used in commercial air conditioning units. Nonetheless, it is a pleasure seeing you," he said trying to sound professional. As he came closer he extended his hand. My mind was whirring, trying to place this guy. I knew him from somewhere! Damn, I wasn't able to figure it out!

"Mr. Gabelli. Dashel," he smiled and I noticed a toothpick dangling from those lips. I took his hand and my mind started trying in earnest to place this guy.

"I'm terribly sorry, Dr. Balzich (damn, that's a funny name!), we have met before?" I asked, squinting at him—as if by distorting my corneas, I might be able to find this guy's face in my memory banks—as I took his hand and shook it for a quick second or two.

He laughed a brief phony laugh and released my hand. "Yes, it was about twenty years ago while I was visiting my Aunt Dorathea here, in Norristown. I was also doing some research at the time."

Now that my mind had a time reference, it began pouring over the filters. Norristown. Research......nothing. The name. Try the name. Franklin P. Balzich. Frank Balzich. Frank Balzich. Frances Balzich. Fran Balzich. Frank P Balzich.....wait a minute...here it comes...Frank B....Frankie B! Holy Shit! It all clicked—the face, the name, the tooth-pick. Frankie B from the Norristown Library! That incredible windbag of a buffoon that spewed unbelievable tales and downright bullshit! Oh, Good Lord, it was him. I imagine the look on my face gave me away that I indeed did now recognize him.

"Frankie B!" I feigned interest in my voice in seeing this guy again, thinking how ironic it was that he was there when I began my research and now that I have completed it, he is here again. Kooky!

"Yes! You remembered! How wonderful! As I recall, you were doing some research in the area of blood disorders, right?"

"No, it is.."

"Wait, wait...don't tell me! Okay, it was about arthritic mice, right?"

"No, it deals with.."

"The effects of asphaltic acids on four ply radial tires! Yes, now I remember! My, that must have been terribly exciting work!"

"No, it has to do with dreams. The effects of foods on my dreams. How by eating certain foods I was able to produce most vividly detailed dreams." I said, a little disappointed that I showed up here. I was also going to mention to him that I didn't think that there any such thing as 'asphaltic acid' but decided against possibly provoking this kook. All of the sudden, he didn't seem at all like a man of science despite the image he was trying to project with his appearance. He just looked like the dope I met back in the library oh those many years back wearing a white lab coat and nerdy glasses.

"Oh yeah. Well, whatever. What can I do for ya?" he asked.

"Well, I don't think..." I tried to get out of here before he started, but it was too late.

"Probably want me to publish your work, huh? Well, that might be a possibility. It depends of course on what you have. Hey, you wanna know what I've been up to since I last saw you?" he now totally reverted to Frankie B, discarding the lab coat and glasses (as I looked closer, I discovered that they did not have lenses) and slipping into his 'I'm getting excited here to tell you a long winded story—hell, maybe a whole bunch of them!' frenzy.

"Sure, why not?" I replied, just giving up now and letting him go, maybe in hopes that he will keep things short and I can get the hell out of here.

I followed him back behind the cheap, closet door to his brightly lit office which was such a contrast form the dark outer area that my eyes hurt a bit. I sensed a headache coming on. Either from the high—power fluorescent lighting or his upcoming monologue, I wasn't sure. I sat down on a metal folding chair in front of a folding card table covered with a plastic table covering depicting "old fashioned" Christmas scenes that served as his desk. On his desk were a few pens sticking out of an old off brand soup can, a spiral bound notebook and a little plastic basket lined with wax paper and filled with chicken wing bones. He went to the other side and sat down on what appeared to be a barstool that had it's legs shortened so it would be the correct height in proportion to the card table/desk. He took another toothpick out of a small box that was in his slightly over worn, flannel shirt pocket, placed it in his mouth, leaned forward over the table, crossed his arms in front him on the table for support, looked at me, winked, smiled, took a deep breath and then he started. Here we go again.

He started by reminding me that he was in the library (yeah, yeah, I know, I was there, you dope) and that he was carted out for talking out loud to himself. I didn't mention to him that I had seen him being thrown out in fear that might make this whole thing that much longer. A few days later, he returned to his "home" in the abandoned salt mine shaft in Hutchinson, Kansas to complete his "mind expansion" studies.

He still considered himself the "Smartest Man in Nebraska" at that time and was in the process in completing a self-developed test to see if he was now smarter than an African Elephant running a high-grade fever caused by mutant strain of German Measles or the country of Mexico. He was also reading heavily about the close genetic relationship that exists between human beings and creatures of the simian family. He briefly mentioned (with his eyes gazing down to the tiled floor of his "office") that he failed his own test, but that failure (his eyes now back up and looking at me again) caused him to delve further into the "magical and really...I mean really, REALLY, interesting connection that we have with monkeys, chimps, apes and believe it or not, baboons!"

I was now beginning to fade in and out of what he was saying and figuring out if I would have time to go home and find myself another publisher (at this point, I didn't really think that Frankie B. was a publisher at all) before the day was over. I glanced at my watch and saw that it was 2:44 pm. Probably not enough time to get home and make some more phone calls by the time this wind bag was done blabbing. Might not even get home by tomorrow, I joked to myself, but didn't find myself laughing at that thought. It might actually be the case. Holy Crap! And on he continued.

He mentioned briefly his old friend, the "Weedboozer" as Frankie B had scientifically classified him way back when he had initially met him at a truck stop. Apparently this gentleman who indulged in booze, crack and whatever was available and affordable on his unemployment check, volunteered for some military science research project and was now living in Thailand. Frankie B didn't feel he was at liberty to discuss with me (I'm betting he had no idea whatsoever) the exact details or of any activities that his friend had been involved in, but he did say that last he heard, he was no longer smoking crack or drinking in excess, but he now had extremely long fingers. He then went on, saying nothing more on the subject, leaving me shaking my head, trying to possibly shake myself into a concussion or to some level of unconsciousness.

He went back to his study of simians and told me that he was most fortunate to acquire a baboon from a facility in a small town near the Oklahoma/Kansas border. "It looked like an abandoned military installation from the outside, but inside was filled with computers and all sorts of ingenious testing equipment! I'm sure that you would appreciate this place!" I nodded, almost a second too late as I was calculating the number of tiles lining the floor in his "office" and how many would be needed if I wanted to tile a direct trail to the Norristown Rehabilitation Center (read: Loony Bin), which was approximately 2 miles away. He droned on.

This baboon was one that the facility (still don't know what type of place just gives away baboons to any half-ass that calls in) readily gave up. Frankie B said that they were happy to see him come and take the animal away. I wanted to ask if that didn't make him in the least bit suspicious, but I knew that if I started asking questions, I would most likely truly be here until tomorrow! Frankie said that the beast was in perfect health but that he was past the prime "testing years." It seems, according to Frankie, that once a baboon (he wasn't quite sure if this rule applied to all simian—type creatures) reaches the age of 20 or so, he no longer has the reflexes necessary to participate in the many tests that require a quick and accurate reaction time. So, Frankie explained, rather than have the poor thing destroyed, the facility makes them available to zoos and the such. However, nearly every zoo in the world has their fill of baboons (even those safari drive through parks where your car becomes the mobile dance floor for these pitiful creatures as they eat vinyl roofs, crap on your windshields, and snap off car antennas) and this one was earmarked to be incinerated. Until Frankie called on a whim and found the beast available. "Talk about luck!" Frankie exclaimed! Yeah. Bad luck. For the poor baboon. He probably would have been better off roasted to ashes and his bones used to manufacture flea market jewelry. This brought a small, audible chuckle from me and the words, "Yeah, you got the luck, Frankie B. Hoo Yeah!"

I again started to wax in and out of the monologue being delivered by Frankie B., jackass of science. I did manage to catch a few things here and there about how he took the baboon and taught it sign language (which kinda impressed me a bit) and "rudimentary math skills" (Frankie said that it was simple addition and subtraction stuff, but I was beginning to be impressed when it dawned on me that he was probably lying or at the least exaggerating to great degree. But he did manage to grab my attention for a bit).

Then Frankie B. informed me that he had been able to teach the creature to drive. Oh Geez, I thought to myself, here we go. But not to drive simple automobiles, pick up trucks, Sport Utility Vehicles, Monster Trucks or Humvees. The creature had been taught how to operate heavy machinery. And not the "ordinary" heavy machinery vehicles like back—hoes, bulldozers, cranes and front—end loaders. He was instructed on how to work a giant piece of machinery that is primarily used in mining operations—those gigantic dump trucks that weigh about 720,000 pounds (and that's with the bed empty). This I gotta hear about!

He went on to explain that he really wanted to teach the baboon he named Felix to work the monster piece of machinery that they use to bring space shuttles out to the launch pad, but that he was not able to find any operating instructions detailed enough for him to build a simulator. Apparently the details were classified information and he would never be able to access them. "Yeah, NASA is funny like that, you know, letting just anyone (kooks like him in particular) have that kind of stuff," I interjected. He ignored my comment and went on to explain how he built a simulator that was an exact duplicate of the interior cab of the latest model of giant dump truck they used at the time. He said that it only took Felix a few weeks to get the procedures—from starting up the behemoth truck, putting it through all the necessary maneuvers and shutting it down at the end of the day.

Frankie B. told me that he wanted to showcase to the world the most amazing skill he had imparted to this filthy animal. He told me that he took Felix into Southern Arizona, to a very large copper mining operation and asked the head of the operation to allow Felix to run the giant truck for just one day. I could just imagine the head of things just up and throwing out this moron and his baboon dressed up to look like an organ grinder's monkey out the window and calling it a day. But, Frankie went on, the chief thought that it would be a great publicity stunt to generate interest in his mining operation (as if anyone really cared anyway) and, after ignoring the loud protests from the driver of the truck that Felix the baboon would be driving (probably fearing that everyone would think lesser of his abilities that had taken him years to accomplish if a flea bitten, filthy baboon was able to do his job), it was agreed that the baboon would drive the truck for one half day to test him and that the next day they would do it again in front of the press.

Felix climbed up to the cap in about 10 seconds (it helps being able to scale the exterior without thought rather than following safe and proven entry procedures designed to keep mere humans from serious injury and/or death) and put on a hard hat. The image of a baboon wearing a hard hat and a little red vest with yellow tassels dangling from it sitting in the cab of a gigantic truck caused me to chuckle again out loud. Frankie didn't notice and continued. Felix started the vehicle, put it in gear and pulled out to a very wide expanse of the open pit mining area where the baboon would be able to show what he was able to do.

Things went very well according to Frankie. Felix was able to operate the vehicle through some very difficult maneuvers and the chief of operations was definitely impressed. As much as he was elated, ALL the regular, human operators of giant dump trucks were beginning to bite their fingernails and chain smoke cigarettes as the fear of losing their "cushy" jobs began to spread like wildfire. The operators of other gigantic mining machines (like the monstrous front end loaders and bulldozers) began to wonder as well. If a filthy baboon could replace the truck drivers, how long before they would be replaced? What if it even doesn't have to be as smart as a baboon? What if they could teach raccoons or such to operate the stuff? Frankie mentioned that he had begun to feel uncomfortable as the stares of some very large men and women we getting to him. For the entire morning (Felix even worked through the regularly scheduled break time- which caused major gripes from the workers, even as they went to take theirs) the animal performed his duties as well as any operator ever could. Frankie mentioned to him in an aside that this would be a tremendous boon to his operation and mining in general. The director was thinking he wouldn't have to deal with unions and he could pay the beasts in bananas or spoiled fruit or whatever the hell it was they ate. It would save millions of dollars! The great smile on the chief's face made Frankie feel better even as the stares of the onlookers had become more piercing and were now occasionally followed by threatening remarks such as "Geez, I would hate to see anything happen to the guy who brought that Goddamn disease carrying, lice infested, monkey here!" and "I think that my prone to fly off the handle wife would probably come here herself and flat out kill anyone who threatened to take food off of our table!" More mutterings included the words "death," "slice him like a loaf of crusty bread," "castration," "flattened beyond recognition," "it would take a 1000 years to find anybody in that one mine" and " that motherfucker is dead!"

Still, Felix plodded on, doing everything that Frankie B had taught him to expect at such a site and how to react to each situation. He managed to make that gigantic truck move like it was on air. All morning long under the bright blue, dry Arizona sky, this baboon known as Felix was doing a job that was previously thought to be relegated to highly trained humans. Frankie B could begin to imagine the press plastering the story and his name all over the world. He would be famous! Hell, he might even win a Nobel Prize! (I couldn't think in what category; I thought they had abolished the "Enslaving and Torturing Beasts for Menial Labor" award a few years back.) He would be asked to chair large research organizations, start think tanks, and be widely sought after to speak at college graduations! Frankie B was on top of the world!

Then it was lunch time. Although Frankie had spent an extraordinary amount of time with Felix teaching him everything necessary to operate the giant truck, he never quite covered the concept of the lunch whistle. Felix had become accustomed to the workplace noises through tapes that Frankie B played over and over again. The sounds of explosions as they blew away sides of mountains, the sounds of metal scraping rock as magnificent shovels dug into the earth, the low, guttural grinding noise from large drilling devices were all commonplace in the brain of the baboon. And not once in all those tapes was there the sound of a lunch whistle. The exceptionally loud, shrill high pitched sound that announced to the hard working men and women that it was now time to put nourishment into those human machines so they can operate at optimum capability for the remainder of the day. Looking back, Frankie B mentions to me that perhaps he should have thrown a couple of whistles in there somewhere along the line. Preferably before he brought Felix to the mining site.

At 12 noon (MST) the regular, everyday occurrence of the lunch whistle screaming came. Frankie B said that it was hard to pinpoint the exact time (perhaps a fraction of a second or two after the whistle he surmised) the Felix lost his baboon mind. Perhaps a second or two before the whistle went off, Frankie B thought to himself, almost a premonition of impending doom, that he forgot to let Felix hear the whistle. He could do nothing, of course, except watch with everyone else what would unfold. And unfold it did.

Even above the loud scream of the whistle, everyone could hear the eerie shrieks coming from the interior of the gargantuan vehicle. The hair on the back of Frankie B's neck stood straight out and goose bumps were visible on the chief's forearm as he shuddered at the noise. The great vehicle (in my mind I was thinking about the Mammoth Car that was in the Speed Racer cartoon series) continued on a direct path to the platform that Frankie B and the chief and assorted other onlookers were assembled. Felix had climbed out of the cab, sort of repelled (like chimps and such who get spooked because some guy with a blow gun is trying to kill them do to get down out from the upper branches of trees) to the ground and simply took off running nearly full on two legs like a human being. He still had that bright yellow hard hat on his baboon head and that snazzy red vest with the yellow tassels on his baboon body as he headed at full lope out of the mine area.

It only took a few moments for all those gathered on the observation platform to disperse as the truck came straight at them at a blistering 5 miles an hour. The words that were aimed at Frankie B muttered from the workers who were in peril of losing their jobs had commenced again and a few additional, just as savory comments were now attributed to the chief of operations. It took about 20 seconds or so (Again, Frankie B was somewhat vague on the timing of this experiment as it was hard to look at your watch as people were threatening to kill you while you were running for your life) for the vehicle to hit the platform, completely destroying the structure, leaving the truck with it's front against the side of the mine trying to continue on it's forward path. As big and powerful as the machine was, it could not push it's way through the mountain.

After the fire and rescue crews had extinguished the flames (from the explosion of the giant truck's massive engine and fuel tanks), Frankie B was summoned to the chief's office. Frankie B said that he was in a daze for most of the brief tirade the chief had spewed, but did manage to hear the words "millions of dollars in damage'" and "I should have you killed when you walked in here with that Goddamn monkey" repeated once or twice in the speech. Frankie B. was escorted out and led to the entrance of the mining operation where he was told that if he was still in the state of Arizona in three hours, he would be hunted down and killed. The chief had made Frankie B promise never to let word of this out or he would be killed wherever he was. The idea that someone would let a baboon operate a complicated piece of machinery would make the chief the laughing stock of the world and of course he would lose his "cushy" job. Frankie B looked at me with somewhat squinted eyes and stopped speaking.

"You're not going to tell this story to anyone are you? It could get me killed!"

While I hesitated in responding for a second or two, pretending that I was actually pondering the thought (for a brief moment it was more than pretending) and replied that of course I would keep it to myself. Who would believe me anyway? I was about to get up and leave, thinking (quite foolishly) that this was over. However, Frankie B said nothing to stop me. But I was curious. What had happened to Felix? Crap, I asked that out loud!

"Well, I am glad you asked," replied Frankie B and proceeded with another story.

The way he told me (from all that I actually listened to), Felix had run out of the mining area and simply disappeared. Frankie B made a beeline back to Kansas and his cozy salt mine home. He said that he heard nothing of anyone seeing a baboon in the area surrounding the mining area or anywhere for that matter. He was a little concerned that perhaps he was eaten by coyotes or simply died, a lab baboon left to the elements. He always thought in the back of his mind that Felix would survive on his own, but that idea waned with time. Then, one night while watching TV, he got some closure.

He was watching the local newscast and right before the weather, there was a story about an occurrence at the Smoky Hill River Festival. Apparently it was something more than the fluff, human interest story about the festival that one would normally expect. Frankie B asked me if I would like to see the news story. He had received a copy of the tape from the television station and was now holding it in his hand. "Sure, why not?" I replied.

Frankie got up and pulled back a curtain behind his folding card table "desk" and revealed a television on a black wheeled stand. A video tape player was located on a lower shelf of the stand. Frankie B put in the tape and used the remote control to start the television (which only showed "snow" indicating that it wasn't set up to receive any actual television programming). In a few seconds the screen turned blue then showed a female reporter wearing a cowboy hat over her red, knotted hair and a serious look on her face.

"The Smoky Hill Festival has always been a wonderful place to bring the entire family to enjoy the clowns that perform magic tricks to entertain the children and easily amused adults, inhale the stench from the animal exhibits, and devour voluminous amounts of slow-roasted corn in the husk and various salt laden snacks. This year there has been a new addition to the usual array of booths showcasing pieces of splintered wood glued together and painted crazy colors that is passed off as crafts and the groups of extremely loud punk musicians that have never had one note of their 'music' played out of the county limits–some not even out of their junk filled garages. This year, in an attempt to bring an aura of class to the Festival, the entertainment board managed to have one of the largest dog shows in the country open an exhibit in the main tent. But things don't always work out the way they are planned."

Video is playing as, in the background, the reporter continues speaking. Images of purebred canines performing various acts of obedience are shown.

"These dogs and their owners have made the trek here to Kansas from their homes located all over the United States and Canada to give the great people who attend this wonderful Festival a glimpse of how 'the other half' live. Dog Shows have typically been associated with well—to—do individuals who have a tad bit too much money and an enormous amount of free time on their hands. While the show here today was intended as a showcase of the elite, what the Festival attendees got was certainly a lot more entertaining."

The video is now focused on a pair of collies and their owner standing in line, waiting to do their tricks. The dogs are panting heavily and whimpering, something not usually associated with these exceptionally trained and well-behaved animals. They began pacing as the reporter continued with the voice over.

"These magnificent dogs are purebred, registered collies and, according to their owner, Arnold Phaltzgraf of Boulder, Colorado, have received advanced degrees from numerous, world renowned canine training facilities. These animals were supposed to be, 'Top of The Class,' but as you'll see, they certainly didn't behave that way today!"

The video now shows the dogs waiting to perform. The owner, Mr. Phaltzgraf, was having a difficult time restraining the animals on their leashes as they have now started jumping up and down and walking in circles. The signal came for them to perform and the dogs were released to perform their repertoire. The dogs ran the length of the plastic turf runway, barking. They started towards the group of dogs who have recently completed their routines. The collies barked and growled at the others then began sniffing their rear quarters. The dogs then ran around the tent with the owner chasing them. The assembled crowd began giggling at first site of this odd display at such a "high falootin'" exhibit and starting howling with torrents of deep laughter, holding their sides, tears running down their cheeks as the dogs began vomiting and defecating at random, howling all the while. The owner slipped in a pile of feces and landed on his back which looked to be quite a painful experience. The laughter turned to cheers, whistles, backwoods hollers and applause as the audience assumed this to be a part of the exhibit. The stern looks on the judges' faces as they approached Mr. Phaltzgraf clearly indicated that it was not.

The female reporter is now on the screen along with Arnold Phaltzgraf. He is wringing his hands and has a worried look on his face.

"I have with me, Mr. Arnold Phaltzgraf from Boulder, Colorado. Mr. Phaltzgraf, this show started as a terrific event and went along real well until your animals took the stage. Could you tell us what happened?"

"Well," began Arnold, still wringing his hands and beads of sweat forming on his forehead, "My babies, Ashley and Romolon, are, well, they are magnificent creatures, they really are. I knew something was wrong after the incident we had on the way here."

"The incident you are referring to happened on Interstate 81, just south of Salina, is that correct? Right past Little Erma's Truck Stop and Lap Dance Center where every Thursday night is all you can eat Crow Legs—available in hot, super hot, and 'Call 911, My Pharynx Has Seized?'"

"Yes, yes, that would be it, I suppose. This, this abomination of behavior spooked me as well as my poor precious babies!"

"Well, before you tell us what happened, let's go take a look at your car," said the female reporter as they both headed to a LeBaron station wagon with wood paneling and a dented rear. It also had one of those stickers that stated: Show Dogs On Board–Please, Don't Honk! "I see that the rear gate area here has some damage to it. Tell us what happened."

"It was horrible! Horrible, I tell you!" started Arnold, virtually in tears, wringing his hands with an extreme vigor, "I was just south of town and I was looking forward to attending the Festival. I had my reservation at first, you know, coming to such a teeny little fair, in a small, backward town, but I thought to myself, 'This could be such a great thing to happen to such a non–town and that this group of socially ignorant people would truly be dazzled' and I was becoming genuinely excited in attending. I had my ABBA tapes playing, the babies love ABBA, and we were singing having a great time! The dogs love to hear me sing such hits as 'Fernando' and 'Dancing Queen.'

"Then all of a sudden, I hear this a loud horn blast from behind the car! It was a tractor-trailer cab and the driver must have been hanging on the horn! It was loud and obnoxious and it was scaring my babies! It kept getting closer and closer, still laying on the horn and the dogs were starting to bark and cry! My poor, poor, babies! It got even closer, real quick! Then he sort of rammed the back of the wagon! Then he roared past me on the left! I nearly soiled myself and the dogs certainly had bowel movements! I had to pull over and give myself a dose of smelling salts and triple filtered Italian mineral water!"

"That's amazing!" exclaimed the female reporter, "Did you get a look of the driver!?"

"Well, uh, yes, yes I did," he said with a hesitancy that indicates that perhaps he would rather not answer this question, "I looked back and, right before I was rammed from behind, I got a perfect look at the driver from the rearview mirror!"

"And you gave a description to the police?"

"Yes, I did. And they threw me out of the station!" exclaimed Arnold.

"And tell us why that is, Mr. Phaltzgraf," asked the reporter, obviously knowing the answer, "and, please, give us a description of the driver so we may be of some help in catching the horrible demon who did this to you and your beautiful, neurotic dogs."

"The police told me that even though they were a small town operation, that I couldn't come in here and play games with them. I just gave them the whole story and a description and then they escorted me out!"

"And what did the driver look like?" again, with the air of knowing the answer.

"Well, I thought it was strange, but I saw what I saw. At first I thought it was a midget—oops can I say that? Maybe the term 'little person' would be more proper. Anyways, it wasn't one of those. The driver of the tractor-trailer cab was a baboon wearing a yellow hard hat, a red vest with yellow tassels and smoking a big cigar. He was hanging on the horn cord, just driving straight ahead. After he rammed me, he took off, speeding past me on the left."

"So, a baboon wearing a hard hat, a red vest with yellow tassels and smoking a cigar was driving a truck cab, rammed you, and then sped away?"

"Yes, yes, that would be a most accurate description of the events that occurred."

"Thank you, Mr. Phaltzgraf," she said as she rolled her eyes skyward and walked away from him and the dented station wagon, "What a strange turn of events. Bye, bye."

"Well, ladies and gentlemen, one of two things is quite evident. Either there exists some sort of unknown virus in Arizona that affects both humans and canines that causes a degree of mental degeneration, or, if you can believe this, someone has managed to teach a filthy animal, like a baboon to drive a very large vehicle. I think we all know the answer to this one. I would also like to mention here that after speaking to the judges, I have found out that Mr. Phaltzgraf has been banned from participating in any future professional dog shows. There has also been discussion of denying him entry to amateur, only partially regulated by the Mafia events. In a sense, his life as he has known is over. Jim, back to you!"

Frankie B raised the remote over his head and pointed it at the television and his the off button. He had a slight smile on his face and just looked at me. "So, there it is. Felix picked up the habit of smoking! You try and try to keep them in line, but, Dammit, they do it to you every time! But, I'm sure he's doing okay. He's probably running a Dairy Queen or a Sonics in Montana or something."

I sat there for a moment wondering if this perhaps was a dream. I shook my head again to clear my head and was about to get out of my chair when Frankie piped up again.

"So, you want to have your stuff published, huh? I think I might be able to help you out. I have published quite a few things over the last few years. My Aunt Dorathea passed and left me a nice sum of money that I used to start this publishing house and place of higher learning. She was taken away from us suddenly and it was a shock, but I'm sure that she would like to have seen me use her funds to further my research."

"I'm sorry to hear of your loss," I said, cordially, "Was she ill?"

"No, not at all! She was as healthy as any 112 year old. She took such good care of herself we thought she would live to be at least 150. She took 127 different vitamin and herbal supplements each day, you see. It would take nearly a whole day just to consume them and they sometimes caused her acute intestinal distention and chronic constipation. But she looked like she was only 90 or so."

Again, I shook my head. I was about to start smacking my head on the card table when Frankie B reached into his back pocket and slid a glossy brochure in front of me. I picked it up and read the front, which stated the name of this wonderful institution, but instead of a picture of this hole in the wall, minimally rehabbed store front, it had a picture of Windsor Castle on the front. I held the brochure up towards Frankie B.

"This is nice, Frankie, but this is a picture of Windsor Castle," I said with a slight grin on my face.

"Yes, I know." replied Frankie B with a serious look on his 50 year old or so face.

"Well, isn't that a bit misleading? I mean, people might think that this is a picture of your facility."

"I'm sorry. I'm not understanding what you're trying to tell me," said Frankie B with a look on his face indicating that he really didn't see that I was implying that he was deliberately trying to mislead people.

"Uh, never mind. Do you have a list of titles you have published?"

"Yes, sir, I do! Open it up and it's on the inside right."

I opened it up and glanced at the left hand side first where there was a list of testimonials. I'll read them a bit later, I thought to myself as I looked to the right side to see the list of titles that were published by Serious Body of Knowledge Press:

A Baboon, A Hard Hat and a Big Dump Truck: The Study of Elevated Levels of Simian Intelligence by Franklin P Balzich, Ph.D.

The Square Wheel: A Study of Common Shapes by Franklin P Balzich, Ph.D.

***Super Mind: How A Smack to the Head With A Sledge Hammer Increases IQ— Provided You're Still Alive*!** by Franklin P Balzich, Ph.D.

Get Out of Here!: A Compilation of Simple Stain Removers by Franklin P Balzich, Ph.D.

Rather than reading on further down the list, I simply had to ask Frankie why he put Ph.D. after his name. Did he have a Master's degree in anything?

"A what?" he asked.

"Well, you have Ph.D. after your name which is used to indicate that you have a Doctorate Degree. What are you a Doctor of?"

"Oh. No, no, you must be mistaken. Ph.D. stands for 'Phonetic Dialectician.' I created my own language, you see, and that's what Ph.D. stands for. May I see what you have to be published?"

I shook my head again and handed him my stack of papers. He quickly looked at the cover page and read out loud, "'THE COMPLETE CHRONICLES OF INVESTIGATIVE STUDY INTO THE EFFECTS OF INGESTED FOODSTUFFS ON THE TOTAL RELEASE OF IMAGINATIVE IMAGES IN ANIMATED, SEQUENTIAL AND EXACTING DETAIL FROM THE SUBCONSCIOUS CAVERNS OF THE HUMAN PSYCHE By Dashel X. Gabelli, Pioneer of Science,' huh? I like it. I'll publish you, if you like."

"But you didn't even look at what I have!"

"Mere formalities, my friend. I think that it'll make a great read. Maybe an even better musical!" stated Frankie B, quite confident and even excited. Something just didn't feel right.

"Would you like a cup of coffee?" asked my most congenial host, Mr. Balzich, Phonetic Dialectician, "I have some already made if you want some. Did I ever tell you that my father invented the first coffee maker? Well, it's true!" Oh geez, I thought, here we go again.

"My father invented quite a few items that others have unabashedly stolen and profited from. Take the automatic drip coffee maker for instance. My father slaved for three years to develop a most amazing machine that would heat the water to brewing temperature, allow it to drip through carefully calculated openings and release perfectly brewed coffee. All the business world laughed at him, saying that his invention would never find it's way into the households of America! Can you believe that?"

"Actually, I find it hard to believe that your father invented the automatic drip coffee maker, and if he did, I would find it even harder to believe that no one would jump all over this invention," I replied, "What reasons did they give him for not wanting to market his machine?"

"Well, he did indeed invent it and I have the original machine located in a warehouse in South Philadelphia. The reason they gave him was that it just wasn't a practical machine."

"Not practical!" I found myself caught up in this banter—though I couldn't figure out why, "How could it not be practical to have a coffee maker sitting on your counter top that all you have to do is put in a couple of scoops of ground coffee and some tap water and then you have a pot of coffee?"

"Well, I personally think it was all a Communist conspiracy, but they gave other petty reasons. First of all, it would never fit on a counter top. The machine was a big as a city block, weighed 37,489 pounds and could only used ozonated water, partially electronically charged with negative ions. It took 37 minutes to brew 2 ½ ounces of coffee. I still, to this day think that it was nothing more than a conspiracy!"

"Yeah, well, you might be right on that," I said as I started to get up out the folding chair, "I don't think it could have anything to do with no one wanting a contraption that weighed nearly 19 tons and made a teeny cup of coffee."

"I think people would have been lined up around the block for it." Stated Frankie B. In my mind I pictured people lined up around a gigantic Mr. Coffee coffee maker with cups in hand waiting for a freakin' cup of coffee.

"Oh yeah, my family made a whole bunch of other things, too! Have you ever heard of the electric toothbrush?" he asked me with a lilting emphasis on the word electric. Before I could muster an answer he continued, "Yes, well of course, a man of science such as yourself probably would have heard of such a thing. My cousin invented this item! Again, rebuked by the business world. He developed a toothbrush that used rebuilt automobile transmissions and industrial turbines and steel bristles to effectively cleanse teeth!"

Hey! I said to myself, that sounded awfully familiar. It wasn't possible that he could have read that little bit in my research about the dream I had with the catalog (I really should start using some sort of scientific labeling or something)!

"Then my half step sister invented something called 'cough medicine.' Ever hear of it? I'm sure that you have now that they stole her formulation and mass marketed the stuff. The stuff nowadays is a little different than what my half step sister had developed. Hers was primarily for animals like horses, mules and such. She had a little trouble with the stuff, though. It caused severe throat inflammation in the beasts and no one could tell what they were saying anymore. Really a shame."

Good Lord! I am a smoker, though I don't smoke that much (kids, don't smoke—and stay in school!) since my body tells me when I have smoked too much. I usually have a coughing fit that causes my head to shake so that I sometimes see little white spots floating around. I was seeing those spots now.

"Did you know that my Aunt Gretchen invented the steak knife? It all happened when she was living in a boarding house in the not so nice part of Houston, Texas. She had taken to raising Norwegian Alpacas for fun and profit. But, she didn't raise them the way everybody else did.

She used a process of animal rearing called 'Monstrification,' which was developed and perfected by my Uncle Bernie. He found that by only minor tinkering with genetic blueprints he could raise gigantic animals and sometimes even flowers and vegetables—oh, you should see the size of the bell peppers he raised last year! One pepper weighed in a nearly 500 pounds. For a publicity stunt, he placed it on a wagon of sorts and had it pulled by three incredibly large ferrets. His process made these normally petite mammals the size of Cadillacs. It seems that the press thought my Uncle Bernie to be somewhat, how did they put it? Oh yes, he was a 'somewhat peculiar gent taken to fits of dementia.' They thought he was a nut. Could you imagine that? " he paused for a brief moment perhaps waiting for a response from me that would never come. He droned on.

"So anyway, she raised these giant Norwegian Alpacas and she is making some decent money, right? Then she gets a call from the Tex-Mex restaurant that she is living over. Now this place is open all night and she had to put up with horrendous shouting sessions in Spanish and what she called 'Chicano Tunes' emanating from the low riders which spent the whole night racing up and down in front of her boarding house. The cops tried to shut them down on several occasions, but, my Aunt Gretchen thinks there was a conspiracy between the scofflaws and the authorities, you know what I mean? The filthy part of town she had lived in was overrun with corruption! She didn't want to say anything, mind you, lest they discover that in her tiny boarding she had six, highly oversized Norwegian Alpacas. But enough was enough! She called the District Attorney and told them that they had to clean up the area. The DA told my Aunt to, get this, 'If you want it cleaned up, clean it up yourself!' Can you believe that nonsense? What the hell was that about? So she hooks up with this guy in a bar where the slum living, urban Latino cowboys drink unrefined corn liquor and smoke crappy, low grade homegrown weed until they can barely see. She takes him back to her room and he sees these gigantic animals, but he's very much out of touch with reality due to his excesses so far that evening. He thinks that he is losing his mind and starts screaming and the people in the streets are hearing in slurred Spanish that 'this place is the zoo of the devil!' and they all climb the stairs in an attempt to storm my Aunt's room. They're carrying small caliber pistols, chains, iron bars and the such when...."

"Wait a minute," I piped in, "How did your Aunt invent the Steak knife?" I had to stop this insanity!

"What?" He seemed to be thrown for a bit. "Oh, yes, the steak knife. What about it?"

"Uh, I forgot I need to buy some steak knives!" I stammered as I rose from my chair, knocking it over as I grabbed my manuscript and started rushing to the exit, "Yeah, I need to go now before all the stores close. Yes, that's it. I'm sure you understand, don't you? Yes, of course you do. Gotta go. Ta-ta. Ciao. Bye bye!"

Epilogue

I managed to escape from the God—forsaken, dilapidated old department store that Frankie B, uh, I mean, Franklin P Balzich, Ph.D. (Phonetic Dialectician my ass), called his office. I nearly knocked the hooker standing right outside on her ass as she nearly was clobbered by the door which was swung open with full force. I ran into the guy playing the xylophone and nearly tripped over the booze hound laying on the sidewalk, apparently still unconscious to his surroundings. I jumped in my car and was home in no time. Now, I had to go and find some way to get this published! I'll worry about that later.

In any event, the material that I have chronicled in the research section of this wonderful read are records of specific dreams that I have had while eating different foods before sleep. Since it only applies to my experience, how can I classify it as scientific research? Well, in sense, it most certainly is since I did studies (the eating, the sleeping and the dreaming) but, I believe that there must be some validation to some degree. So, how do I validate what I have done? Have the experiments duplicated by someone else.

And who would be sufficiently lacking in the mental arena enough to take on the arduous burden of the research I have conducted. I don't know. I was kinda hoping that you would help me in that area. Now, It doesn't have to be a gargantuan undertaking on your part. Look, as a human being, you eat and you sleep. Yeah, I know you do other stuff as well, but that other stuff you couldn't do if you didn't eat and sleep. I'm right, aren't I? Of course, I am. When I'm right, I'm right. That's right, so sit back down in your chair and keep reading. Punk.

So, this is what you do. Pick a day (any day will do unless of course you have some religious restriction which prevents you from eating and sleeping on a particular day or season of the year. Don't laugh, there probably are some) and make plans to have a very large, very heavy dinner (or supper as some people call it—just think of it as the last meal of the day, for crying out loud!) relatively close to when you plan to sleep. Now, it doesn't have to be a full night's sleep. A nap will suffice. And everyone enjoys a nap after consuming massive amounts of food! And if you keep the television on, all the better! And just keep repeating to yourself that you want to have a vivid dream—color, sound, texture, smells, the whole nine yards! Then just doze off.

Now, when you're having your dream, make a conscious effort to remember what is taking place in your head. It really isn't that difficult. So, shut your mouth with all your complaining, "Oh, I just bought a book to read. I'm not going to do anything for this guy! He's making a mint off this shit anyways! No way in hell am I gonna do it! Eat all that food before bed! What is he? Out of his fuckin' mind? That'll kill you! That crazy son of a bitch wants to kill us all!! Oh, man, that shit just ain't right!" and your crying and sobbing! Just do it and you will be presently surprised at the outcome!

It had occurred to me that perhaps I should ask you to record your dreams and forward them to me. You know, to have the validation thing, but then I would have to read them. And besides being lazy, I know some of you and I know you can't write for crap. Where would I keep all the stuff anyways? That's all I need. 25,000 dreams that are sloppily written and don't make any sense (grammatical and otherwise) since they would be not complete and half will just be made up nonsense—just like those letters that you read in Penthouse Magazine! And they would have to be VIVID and detailed! Not just the, "Yeah, I saw this chick, she was like, my old girlfriend, right, then, I don't know, we take a trip to the mountains, I think, and then, no wait a minute, it was trip to Mexico, yeah, Mexico and we had a tiny hotel room, right, then, no wait it was in Canada, right, Canada—they have the flag with the red leaf in it, right? So, we go on this trip and, she's like, you know 'I think we should have never broke up,' right, then the maid, comes in to bring some towels or food, right, then, no, wait a minute, hold on, did I say I thought it was an old girlfriend? No, no, no, it was Cher, you know when she was with Sonny and Cher, and she's singing and we're in Vegas, that's the place, Vegas. So, she's wearing a turban and a towel and she has dark sunglasses on and she asks if I want a shrimp cocktail, right, so I sat 'yeah, sure,' no wait, I'm allergic to shrimp, makes my head plump up like a ham. My friends used to call me 'ham face' when I was a kid since I had had that reaction on more than one occasion. Even lobster. You know that a lobster is nothing more that a cockroach that lives underwater? True, saw some preacher talk about it on one of those begging for money churches. Anyways, Cher comes over and…" You get the picture, I'm sure!

But, if you do take to experimentation in this area, can write at a third or fourth grade level, and can provide a detailed accounting of a dream which you incurred after a particular combination of food, I would like to see it. So I can steal it and use it for later books. No, that would be silly. Well, not so much silly as , say, illegal! Bottom line—you want to, send it in.

Alright, so all you have to do is eat, sleep, dream and then write it down. And May God Have Mercy On Your Soul.

Boy, this would make on hell of musical, wouldn't it?